Praise for Tanya Anne Crosby's National Bestseller, *The Girl Who Stayed*:

"A beautifully written, page-turning novel packed with emotion."
– #1 *New York Times* bestselling author Barbara Freethy

"*The Girl Who Stayed* is a deeply moving story. I am fascinated by the concept and by Tanya Crosby's stunning storytelling."
– Stella Cameron, *New York Times* bestselling author

"*The Girl Who Stayed* defies type. Crosby's tale is honest and sensitive, eerie and tragic. It's a homecoming tale of a past ever with us and irrevocably lost forever. A haunting vision of that chasm between life and death we call 'missing.'"
– Pamela Morsi, bestselling author of *Simple Jess*

"An intense, mesmerizing Southern drama about a young woman who returns to her coastal home to put to rest the haunting ghost of her sister's tragic past. Told in the rich, lyrical style of Siddons and Conroy, *The Girl Who Stayed* is a woman's story of discovery and acceptance, redefined by Tanya Anne Crosby's dramatic storytelling, sharp characters, and well-defined plot. A must read for any woman who believes she can never go back home. Fabulous, rich, and evocative!"
– *New York Times* bestselling author Jill Barnett

"Crosby tugs heartstrings in a spellbinding story of a woman trying to move beyond her past."
– *New York Times* bestselling author Susan Andersen

"In one word, exceptional!"
– *Literarily Illumined*

Redemption Song

REDEMPTION SONG

TANYA ANNE CROSBY

THE STORY PLANT

This is a work of fiction. Names, characters, places, and incidents either are the product of the author's imagination or are used fictitiously. Any resemblance to actual events, locales, organizations, or persons living or dead is entirely coincidental and beyond the intent of either the author or the publisher.

Studio Digital CT, LLC
P.O. Box 4331
Stamford, CT 06907

Copyright © 2017 by Tanya Anne Crosby
Jacket design by Barbara Aronica Buck

Story Plant Hardcover ISBN-13: 978-1-61188-249-0
Fiction Studio Books E-book ISBN-13: 978-1-945839-11-5

Visit our website at www.TheStoryPlant.com

All rights reserved, which includes the right to reproduce this book or portions thereof in any form whatsoever except as provided by U.S. Copyright Law. For information, address The Story Plant.

First Story Plant hardcover printing: January 2018
Printed in the United States of America

0 9 8 7 6 5 4 3 2 1

To my own mami, Isabel, whose birth city, Jerez, inspired *Redemption Song*, and who instilled in me not merely a love for all things Spanish, but a love for storytelling as well. *Madre mia, tu eres mi luz.*

And also to my husband, Scott Thomas Straley, whose love inspires every story I tell.

> To get back up to the shining world from there
> My guide and I went into that hidden tunnel,
> And following its path, we took no care
> To rest, but climbed: he first, then I—so far,
> through a round aperture I saw appear
> Some of the beautiful things that Heaven bears,
> Where we came forth, and once more saw the stars.
> – Dante Alighieri, *Inferno*

Pinoccaia

LIFE ISN'T FAIR.

Or, as Caía's friend Lucy from Athens, Georgia, used to say, "Life ain't been fair, girlfriend." But who ever said it was?

To the contrary, how many times had Caía heard these precise words: "Life. Isn't. Fair." And put more eloquently yet, "If life were fair, they wouldn't make wheelchairs."

Even so, Caía dared to defy the maxim. Why not? She had been profoundly happy as a child, experiencing life on a marvelous scale of superlatives. As an only child, she had been the "best" at everything. Her mother had pinched her cheeks so often she could still feel the sensation, like a muscle memory, flesh trapped firmly between thumb and knuckle—mostly the right cheek because her mom was left-handed.

"Caía, my dear, you are so lovely I could eat you up," she would say, and with such ardor Caía couldn't help but believe it. And, of course, such an intense declaration would naturally lend itself to a frightful duality, for while Caía was intensely pleased to be "so lovely," she didn't want to end up in her mother's belly, again. But having exited said region once already, it remained a dreadful possibility. And sometimes her mom's cute aggression would come in various other iterations, such as, "Caía, you are so smart I can die," or, "Babisiu, you are so sweet I will not bear it."

Of course, Caía didn't want her mother to die, so maybe "smart" should be kept under wraps? And "sweet," while it had a far less frightening trade-off, she could do without that, as well. And yet, for all this magnificent devotion, Caía had begun to believe herself immortal—at least she had until she'd turned ten and soon thereafter discovered her nose was growing at a faster pace than the rest of her face, a small detail she'd discovered through Robbie Bowles on the day he'd nicknamed her Pinoccaia.

Get it, Jack? Caía plus Pinocchio equals Pinoccaia. What a clever little bastard.

The nickname sent Caía home sobbing to her pop, with said nose as rufous as a beet. Mostly because Robbie Bowles had been a cute boy Caía had crushed on forever, and on that hideous day Robbie had revealed to her the unthinkable: that Caía was neither perfect nor immortal. So, of course, she was devastated. All the proof she'd ever need that she was but a hapless mortal lay in the unendurable truth: Robbie's taunts hurt so badly, Caía feared she could and would die over the heartache she'd suffered that day. What was more, she'd feared she might do it right there on the dirty gray floor of her fourth-grade class.

"You are half Polish," her sensible father had explained when Caía returned home from school, tears burning her cheeks. "You have a perfectly good nose, Caía. You will grow into it someday." He had that no-nonsense way about him, and although Caía sensed he was moved by her tears, he would never have allowed her to wallow in self-pity.

Her baba had been Polish, he'd reminded her, and Caía was named after her, albeit with one important distinction: Caía Alicja Nowakowa was an "owa," because she'd been a widow, and Caía was Nowakówna, because she was not yet wed. That she would never graduate from being an *ówna* to an *owa* had never occurred to Caía any more than it had to wonder over her own lack of perfection. Such was the nature of being an only child, delivered to older, first-generation immigrants, who so readily showered their one and only bundle of joy with all their foundling hopes.

Well, so, her father assured her that the first Caía—Caía's grandmother—had had a fine face and a decorous nose that, while not particularly on the delicate side, most folks considered refined. And it was, Caía was forced to agree, as she'd studied the black-and-white portrait her mom kept on the dining room sideboard. With pale yellow hair, and frail shoulders wrapped in a rich fur shawl, her father's mother stared back at her from the depths of the photograph with a serenity that Caía knew in some unerring place in her heart that it must come from a bone-deep assurance that no matter what troubles life would hurl your way, life was, indeed, quite fair.

"Hold your head high," her mother had chided. "Jak cie widza, tak cie pisza." *How they see you, that's how they perceive you.* And so, armed with this attitude, Caía dismissed the Robbie Bowleses of the world. She set her sights on the distant horizon, because she'd always understood there would be more to life than what was awaiting her there in Athens, Georgia. She was fabulous with languages, her mother said. So, perhaps, she might even become an interpreter someday. Or the ambassador to Poland? But, then, that would be a smart thing to do.

Eventually, as her father promised, Caía grew into her fine nose, one that was likened on many occasions to Helen Mirren's. Slightly pointed, long and straight, by the time she was twenty, her nose was no longer too big for her face.

She went on to marry Gregg Paine, the star quarterback of her high school football team, despite the fact that Gregg firmly believed a wife's place was in the home. *Poof.* There went Caía's dreams of becoming the ambassador to Poland, but it didn't matter; she was over the moon—even more so once they'd placed her newborn baby in her arms.

That's you, Jack.

Perfect nose. Ten toes. Ten fingers. So tiny and fabulous.

Jack Lawrence Paine was everything Caía had ever dreamt of as a mom, and not even the inequitable fact that she couldn't seem to bear any more children diminished her joy. Life was, as her father proclaimed it would be, as her son was . . . inherently perfect.

But then she woke up one morning, at the age of thirty-four, despairing, and so full of loathing that even the sky was darkened by its potency. She was so angry, in fact, that anger didn't properly express the superlative nature of her fury. She was incandescently furious—and willing to kill over it—because, goddamn it, life was so goddamned unfair.

But then, who ever said it was?

One

The truth will set you free,
but first it will piss you off.
– *Gloria Steinem*

JERÉZ, SPAIN, PRESENT DAY, 3:12 P.M.

THERE HE WAS. *Right on time.* Walking down the street with that pretty little girl, wearing her lime-green dress and those bright red sneakers. It was impossible to miss those happy colors. *And what was he wearing?* Jeans and a faded blue T-shirt—all laid back and punchy as though he hadn't a care in the world. When was the last time Caía had worn anything but black?

How was this possible? The girl was clinging to him, trusting him to keep her safe. But how could anyone trust that man? What about him was remotely trustworthy?

Like a Nazi, he was hiding here in this sunny little village in southern Spain. But, then again, wasn't this appropriate? He, the escaped villain; Caía, the harbinger of justice . . . although what justice should entail, Caía didn't yet know.

She focused her attention on the varicolored pair, attempting to ignore the swarming pigeons. Some were perched upon the crenellations of an ancient, ruined fortress next to the coffee shop. Some hopped about, pilfering droppings from customers at Rincon Escondido—a small sidewalk café nestled along the path Caía knew he would take.

Over the past few weeks, she'd studied his schedule, knew exactly where he would go and at what time.

Oblivious to the potential nuclear fallout of Caía's wrath, old men dressed in black defied modernity, with bolero hats tipped slightly forward, shielding wrinkled old eyes from a ruthless afternoon sun. All the while sucking on unfiltered cigarettes, they baked themselves from the inside and out, putting out lung fires with baby cervezas.

Seated near the pigeon-infested fountain, a busker strummed his guitar beneath the shade of an orange tree. He stopped now and again to pluck up a cigarette he'd left burning at the edge of the fountain and slip the butt between his lips, sucking hard, before putting it down again to return to his guitar. He looked pleased with himself as he exhaled, putting nearly as much attention into his smoke work as he did his music.

All the while, black-clad servers with moist brows bustled to and fro, sliding cafélitos and small plates onto nearby tables. But, hey, at least no one was ogling their phones.

Distracted, or more like pretending at distraction, Caía tore a fleshy bite from the bollo in her bread basket. Crumbling it between her fingertips, she scattered the spongy bits alongside her table, watching in her peripheral as a fat, greedy pigeon rushed forward for a feast. But she never took her eyes off the man walking down the street.

Who was the girl?

Smiling, the child skipped along beside him, and seeing them together made Caía's face burn hotter than the glowing tip of the busker's cigarette.

Fury welled up inside her, so utterly potent in its incarnation that she had to suck in a breath. Tears pricked at her eyes. Anger stemmed the flow.

He shouldn't get to walk any child across any street, most certainly not that child. He shouldn't get to hold her little hand—or be the recipient of her sweet, innocent glances upward.

God help her, the sight of that child's innocent smile threatened to empty Caía's heart of all its animosity . . . except . . . she couldn't let it go.

No. She wouldn't.

Jack would never again get to look at anyone that way.

Jack. Jack. Jack. Jack.

She repeated the name like a litany in her head, as though she were in danger of forgetting it altogether. Right here and now, she longed to shout out his name—test the sound upon her lips. *Jack!* she wanted to scream. Would he turn around? And did he remember her son's name?

My sweet, sweet Jack, Caía lamented silently.

How long had it been since she'd spoken his name out loud? *Too, too long.* And maybe she never would again. That possibility burned like acid in her gut. Because now who was left to hear what she had to say about Jack? Two short years, and people already turned away whenever she brought him up, casting sidelong glances at her that said, "Caía, oh, Caía, aren't you over him yet?"

No.

I am not.

I will never be over you, Jack.

But maybe that's not what they were thinking at all. Maybe it was really their own discomfort over not being able to change the inalterable truth: Everyone dies. Even babies with their whole lives left to be lived. Even that little girl. Even Jack.

Or perhaps it was more like this: With kids of their own— especially ones who were struggling to maintain a grip on innocence—maybe it was a bit like peeping into Snow White's mirror? "Mirror, mirror on the wall," she could hear them all say. "Who's the saddest, most pathetic parent of all?"

"Why it's still Caía Paine," the mirror would reply. "But beware . . ."

At this point, both of Caía's parents were gone. Gone—a euphemism for dead. But dead was dead. And yet, there must be a bright side to being six feet under. Neither of her parents would ever get to witness a world without Jack. Bleak, empty—so at odds with the bright blue day, with all the twittering birds. *And all that laughter.*

The lady at the table behind Caía giggled, and the easy chatter that followed gave her a stab of envy—an ugly sensation that cast shadows over the powder-blue day. Like a dirty chimney, the smoldering exhaust of her anger obscured the sun, spreading despair and lowering clouds until they pressed firmly against the pate of her head. Speaking too softly for Caía to hear actual words, their tone nevertheless said it all. They were lovers, flirtatious and familiar. Another stab of envy—and anger—accosted her. She was a great big ball of fury—a hot mass, burning like the sun.

No, her anger was more like a tsunami, threatening to devastate everything within its path. Gathering far at sea, it nevertheless gained momentum, like a cyclone, powering toward an indeterminate shore. When and where—and how—it would descend, Caía had no way of knowing. All she knew right now was that every day that passed without relief only made the impending disaster more terrifying. Because there he was. *That man.* Walking that sweet kid across a busy street, without a care in the world. So damned full of himself that he was oblivious to everyone around him. Certainly, he had never noticed Caía—not once.

She watched as he led the child across the street. Cars crawled past on the narrow road, so slow she imagined their tires melting into the gaps between hot cobblestones.

It could happen now, as the girl lifted her red sneaker onto the curb and the heinous thought made Caía's heart hurt.

Symbolically, she picked up the newspaper she'd been reading and rolled it up, twisting it at its center. This was her soul now. Wrung dry. Every time she watched that man walk that child across the road... a little more of her humanity was squeezed away. Because in her mind, she heard the screams of passersby—or maybe they could be her own? She imagined again that terrible thud, the sound of metal crunching bones. She could hear it plainly, and saw it as clearly as though she had been there...

But you weren't there, were you, Caía?

In fact, no, she wasn't around to see the sun winking against a silver bumper stained with blood. *Jack's blood.* Her sweet little boy.

Jack. Jack. Jack. Jack.

Pinching the bread cruelly, Caía hurled more bits onto the sidewalk, keeping her eyes fixed upon the man and the child.

The girl turned another adoring smile up at him, laughing over something he said, and she suddenly jerked her hands free, clapping them together, and Caía's heart leapt into her throat. But that man—yes, she knew his name—seized her hand back.

So, now you pay attention.
Now it matters to you that cars are screaming past.

Except, no they weren't. *Not here.*

More screams battered Caía's brain, but these were screams of anguish. And yes, they were her own. An image blinked out from the depths of her consciousness, a ferocious but frightened blood-spattered face, with pale blue eyes peering out from the veiny cracks in a bathroom mirror.

Violently thrusting the memory aside, Caía sat back, watching the pair escape, all the while voices shrieked in her head. *Oh, my God, Caía! What have you done? Don't move.*

And then, in the background, she'd overheard her husband's frantic conversation with 911, distorted by a Xanax-induced high. *Hurry! It's my wife. She's . . . bleeding.*

Caía swallowed. Maybe it had been right for Gregg to put her away, but she hated him for it nonetheless. The truth was that Caía didn't quite trust herself, even now. Certainly, she didn't want to see that little girl get hurt, but she did want him to suffer—as Caía had suffered. She wanted him to cry and scream and moan, and beat his head against a wall, railing all the while about the injustice of it all. "Life isn't fair!" she wanted him to scream.

No, it wasn't. By God, it wasn't.

And, yes, okay, so maybe she did want him to have to go identify that child's body. She wanted him to cry himself to sleep every night. Every. Night. She wanted him to refuse to eat and lose twenty pounds, so all his friends would worry about his health.

She wanted him to sicken his partner with overwhelming and endless grief, and then she wanted everyone to abandon him for what he couldn't forget.

But how could anyone expect Caía to forget? Really, how did one carry a baby in her belly for nine whole months, watch him grow, year after year—thirteen to be exact—and then just . . . forget? *How do you do that?* How did you change diapers, buy little shoes, pinch toes . . . ?

"How do they feel, Jack?" she remembered asking him when Jack was three. The memory was as clear as the Mirren-ish nose upon Caía's face.

"Good," he'd said, clapping his little hands.

Of course, it was "good." As it always had been for Caía, everything was always good for Jack. He was a bright, carefree child.

"Hmmm," she'd said, examining those brand-new sixty-dollar sneakers. They were fire-engine red. "I don't think there's enough room, Jack."

He would outgrow them in but a few short months, at most. Even at half off, they were still expensive. As much as they had loved her, her thrifty old-world parents would never have splurged for pricy brand-name shoes for a three-year-old, especially since he was bound to outgrow them so soon. Caía might have considered herself a bit more spendy, but she still had an awful lot of her parents' frugality. When she and Gregg went looking for houses in Chicago, Caía had been drawn to the more modest homes in Roscoe Village, fixer-uppers that needed TLC. It was Gregg who'd insisted their neighbors all be white.

"I wike dese, Mommee!" Jack's excitement was evident in his rosy little cheeks.

Caía had pursed her lips then, trying not to grin, wholly resigned to buy her son the sneakers, whatever the cost. But she peered up at the saleswoman and asked, "Do you have these in a seven, please?"

The woman shook her head. "No, sorry. That's all there is . . . what you see here on the rack . . ."

Beside her, Jack did a little dance of joy, if you could call it dancing. He looked like a toddler jogging after a tangle with tequila. Once again, he said, "I wike dese, Mommee!" Fist closed, all his heart in the declaration.

Of course, any resistance Caía might have contemplated crumbled on the spot. "Okay," she'd said, relenting. And she'd smiled up at the saleswoman, and said, "We'll take them."

"How could anyone say no to that sweet little face?" the woman replied. "He's so adorable, I could just eat him up."

Apparently, wanting to eat up children and puppies, and anything else too cute to bear, was a thing—a scientific thing. Caía read somewhere that a researcher at Yale had discovered—by what means she had no idea—that these dimorphic expressions were a helpful tool for parents in helping them constrain out-of-control emotions.

Unfortunately, nothing could help Caía control the fury she was feeling now. And only now did she realize that she should have learned to say no. Gregg should have said no. Nobody had ever said no.

The lime-green dress was scarcely visible now amidst a sea of earth tones. No longer bound by business suits, Nick Kelly had traded his Chicago streets for cobbled lanes and modestly dressed men and women, strolling to and from a mercado, instead of the Mercantile Exchange. Straining to see through the gray, Caía lost the pair when a tall, willowy Spanish woman swept into view, wearing a swingy red Gitana skirt that effectively obscured the last trace of green.

Caía sat back, frowning. So, that was that. Her job was done for the day, her raison d'être complete until 8:45 a.m. the following day, when she would once again make her way to the plaza beside Colegio la Sala Santiago. And there, she would wait until he arrived to walk the girl into her class, and then she would wait, again, here at this café to watch them pass in the afternoon.

For more than three weeks this had been Caía's schedule—simply observing, mind you. This was all she was doing. In fact, she liked to think of herself as a private investigator, despite no one paying her to do the job. She was good enough to be one, because, after all, she had located Nick Kelly here against all odds. He'd left no forwarding address, no client number, nothing.

"I'm sorry, miss," the receptionist had said when Caía worked up the nerve to call his office. "What did you say your name was?"

"Beth Smith," Caía lied, because there must be a million Beth Smiths living in or around the Chicago area. At least one of them must have been Nick Kelly's client.

"I'm sorry, Nick Kelly is no longer with us. But I can transfer you to Sam Starr, if you'd like. He's taking Mr. Kelly's clients."

Sam Starr? What kind of a name was Sam Starr?

Sometimes, it seemed to Caía as though names might be labels—as though God—or one of his administrators, filed people into categories. *Starr, yep. He'll be successful. Give him everything he wants. Paine. Nope. Poor thing. Go ahead, kill her son.*

"Uh, no, thank you," Caía had said politely, and hung up the phone.

Undeterred, she'd sent Nick Kelly an email that bounced back with a message to please direct all future correspondence to *s.starr@starrwealthmanagement.co*. And then she'd sent an actual letter—the kind that couldn't be marked as spam—on the off-chance someone might know where to deliver it. For all intents and purposes, Nick Kelly had vanished so swiftly that by the time Caía was released from the hospital, there was no sign of him, except for the For Sale sign in his front yard. Well, she took that number down, and called. And called. And called. Disguising her voice every time, she'd called until she'd gathered enough information to deduce where he'd gone. Lying was so easy, once you realized it's what you had to do. So, here she was . . . across an ocean, and she still hadn't quite figured out what to do . . .

Where do we go from here, Jack?

A junky silence was her answer. Cars buzzed past. Bicycle bells rang. Women chattered. The busker played on. But the one thing Caía needed to hear—her son's voice, even if it was only in her head—was missing, leaving her with a deafening silence.

Please, Jack . . .

Caía blinked her tears away, focusing on her mission. The girl might be Nick Kelly's daughter, but she looked nothing like him. Besides, Caía had no reason to believe he had ever had a wife or child. Somehow, despite everything, he didn't seem the sort of guy who acquired one without the other, mostly because he didn't seem the type to leave anything to chance. He would carry a rubber with him, always. He would make sure his girlfriend stayed on the pill. And he might even ask before sex, every single time, "Honey, did you take your pill?"

So, of course, he would be selfish and self-concerned. Children wouldn't fit into his "plan." He would have a neat, clean house, with servants to polish his hardwood floors. Brazilian hardwood, no doubt, because he wouldn't care about the environment, or the legalities of obtaining it. And then he would keep his cell phone right up his ass so he never missed a call.

But . . . if all this were true, who was that child?

Sweat trickled between Caía's breasts, and a cold, damp film materialized above her upper lip. It was blistering hot today—too hot to think.

"¿Algo más?" the waiter asked.

Caía turned her gaze up to meet the waiter's dark eyes, plucking her blouse away from her damp flesh. "Gracias, no," she said, and laid a guilty hand over the rolled-up newspaper she had twisted in anger.

The waiter smiled, indicating the bowl in front of her. It was still full of gazpacho and probably tasted wonderful, but

Caía had barely touched it. "Delicioso," she lied, and added, "So good I will be back again tomorrow."

The waiter furrowed his brow.

That's right, she would come again mañana. And every day thereafter. She didn't know what she was going to do, but she was compelled to do something. *For Jack's sake.* For the time being, this was it. This was her cowardly, screwed-up way of dealing with her son's death.

Caía pushed the bowl away, and the waiter took it, setting it alongside the table to brush the crumbs from Caía's tabletop into her wasted soup. Pigeons waddled about his feet, and he glanced up through dark lashes to meet Caía's gaze, as though to scold her for the congregation. There were at least six pigeons now, waiting for more crumbs. "Son como ratas," the waiter groused, locking eyes with Caía as he finished wiping her table.

Caía nodded, realizing only belatedly that she had lured them into the café from the fountain. Son como ratas, he'd said. *They're like rats.*

Gathering up her purse and her newspaper, Caía ducked inside to pay her tab, and then she made her way over to the fountain.

The stone fount was empty. There were droppings all over it. One lone bird shat as Caía watched and scooted over to unveil its dubious artwork. The busker smiled up at Caía, winking as he snatched his cigarette, and Caía turned away, annoyed by the puffs of smoke that wafted up into her face.

She'd read in the paper that they were installing bird feeders with Nicarbazin, a form of birdie birth control to control the population. City council members had originally advocated rounding up the birds and shooting them—a far more immediate answer to their problem.

She imagined Nick Kelly at the end of a shotgun barrel, and the image made her neck tight. *Now, he was a rat. And what do you do with rats? You exterminate them.*

Two

Anger is a brief madness.
– *Horace*

CHICAGO, THURSDAY, JUNE 9, 2016
NICK

"NICK . . . SOME PERSON KEEPS CALLING AND WON'T LEAVE A MESSAGE."

Nick Kelly rolled his chair back from his desk—a Parnian with a hundred-thousand-dollar price tag. It was the ultimate power desk, and the desk, more than the location of his office, broadcasted his partner track. "Some person?"

"A woman, the same one."

"How do you know it's the same woman, Amy?"

His secretary arched perfectly shaped brows. "Because, Nick, I recognize her voice."

Annoyed by her sarcasm, Nick fished a set of keys out of the top desk drawer and stood, slipping them into his trouser pocket. He eyed Amy as he pushed his chair beneath his desk. Would she have bothered mentioning the caller if it had been a man? *Likely not.* Repeated phone calls weren't an anomaly in this line of business. "I asked you to hold my calls, so just keep asking." He lifted his jacket off the back of his chair. Australian navy merino wool by Ermenegildo Zegna, also with a price tag that would make his Irish Catholic mother cross herself twice. It was getting snug. "Eventually, she'll leave a message," he said, struggling to put the jacket on.

"Where are you going?"

Nick lifted a thumb to his temple, pressing hard. If he was annoyed with anyone, it was more himself. "Lunch," he said.

Amy followed him out of the office, into a sea of cubicles. "Will you be back?" She sounded worried, and he made the mistake of turning and looking at her. Her emotions were on the verge of unraveling, but to her credit, she held it together, expressing what she could through her pretty green eyes.

"Not today," he said, and turned away, feeling her eyes bore into his back. But now he felt like an ass. How had he ever allowed himself to get involved? Maybe he'd believed she could be the one to pull him out of his funk? *Stupid move.*

At this point, he'd accomplished everything he'd ever set out to do in life, and at thirty-seven, there wasn't much left on his bucket list. He had a brand-new 7-series BMW—two days old—a house in Roscoe Village, a firm willing to make him a partner in less than a year . . . but he had to go and put it all at risk.

What the hell are you doing?
Living, because you can?

He quit the office, with all its ringing, dinging phones and moved toward the elevator. Before stepping inside, his cell phone rang, and he fished it out of his pocket, answering, though not before checking the caller ID. It was his sister-in-law. Without a word, he hung up again, returning the phone to his pocket, unwilling to talk to Marta while he was in an elevator surrounded by people.

"Damn it," he said.

"You're a wanted man," joked his elevator companion.

Nick turned to meet the man's gaze—a coworker he didn't know by name. "Yeah?" he said, and otherwise held his tongue, because he recognized the look in the guy's eyes. He was just a kid, maybe twenty-two, looking up to Nick the same way he'd once looked up to his dad. But Nick didn't deserve veneration any more than his father had. How true it was that the apple didn't fall far from the tree. Except in Jimmy's case. His brother had turned out to be the better man, living life without reproach. If people got what they deserved, it would be Jimmy living the high life, not him.

He stared down at his shoes. Marco Vittorio. For fuck's sake, he didn't even want to think about the price.

The elevator doors slid open and Nick stepped out, putting his power stride to good use. It had the distinct advantage of discouraging conversation. Anyone who spotted him with this gait immediately understood he was a busy man—too busy to stand around gabbing. He had things to do, it said, places to be, although, in reality, he had nothing on his plate at all. No lunch dates. No fuck dates. No business appointments. *Nothing. Zip. Zilch.* He simply couldn't sit in that chair an instant longer.

Outside, he took his cell phone back out of his pocket, unlocked the screen, and returned Marta's call, placing a hand to his ear so he could hear her.

"Nico," she said, answering on the first ring.

"What is it, Marta?"

She was sobbing.

"Jimmy?"

"Yes," she said, still crying.

Nick's shoulders tightened. He stopped walking, smashing the phone against his ear. For a long moment, he couldn't speak, because he was afraid of what she was trying to say. He stared at the brick-and-mortar building, focusing on a long, wide crack in the brick. Even the sturdiest foundations eventually cracked. Nothing lasted forever.

"Please come..."
"To Spain?"
"Sí."
"I don't know, Marta. I'll try."
"But you must," she insisted.
"What about Jimmy?"
"He will be furious, but I need you."
"Yeah, all right, I'll see what I can do," he said and hung up, slipping the phone back into his trouser pocket. For a moment, he stood, staring down again at his shiny Italian leather shoes, uncertain what to do. And then he turned and made for the parking garage with a sack of sharp nails sitting in the pit of his gut. He wasn't hungry. It was too early for alcohol, so he opted, again, for endorphins, ready to punish his body and shut down his mind.

Resuming his power stride, Nick sliced through a sea of faces, ignoring every one. Eyes, noses, mouths stretched into amorphous lines of kaleidoscopic flesh.

~

JERÉZ, PRESENT DAY

Caía leaned against the old brick wall of the corner super mercado, where she meant to buy coffee—American coffee, not that Spanish variety. Every café in this city served java that was far stronger than she was accustomed to, and this was the only market she knew of that carried a brand she recognized. It also so happened to be across the street from Nº 5 Calle Lealas.

Of course, Caía had a right to shop where she pleased. Simply because this shop faced that house didn't make one bit of difference. For the time being, this was her city as well.

On the other hand, what might be more inauspicious was the simple fact that she'd come forty-five minutes early, before the mercado was due to open its doors.

And perhaps more impugning, she was standing here puffing away on a nasty cigarette, because it gave her a reason to loiter. And she didn't even smoke. If that wasn't enough to make her rethink her motives, she didn't know what was.

It was one thing to wait at a public location, with the expectation that someone might walk by—or even if you knew they would walk by. It was yet another thing to case someone's house like a cat burglar. Private investigations aside, the act of doing so gave Caía a twisty knot in the pit of her gut. But here was her quandary: She was convinced Nick Kelly was a bad guy, and she wanted desperately for him to have to look her in the eyes and acknowledge what he'd done.

She wanted him to tell her that he hadn't been sending trade orders, or texting some bimbo as he ran over her son. So maybe that was all she was looking for? *Closure.*

Before leaving Chicago, Caía had asked around about him. She understood exactly what sort of man Nick was: He was a user. He accepted money from clients, promising returns on investments he couldn't guarantee. Then again, all those Merc traders were sharks, weren't they? One way or the other, whatever Nick Kelly was doing here, Caía couldn't believe it was anything good.

She eyed the house across the street. There was something surreal about the eighteenth-century house seated beneath the old maple's dappled light. Something timeless and lovely. Something that softened the edges of her anger, even as it roused her resentment.

The morning sky matched the salmon paint. The color contrasted nicely with the intense black ironwork on the upper balconies and windows—three upstairs, one below.

She already knew whose house it was.
Marta Herrera Nuñez.

Caía had deduced as much from the mailbox, a nicely engraved, permanent plaque. Presumably, Marta was the mystery child's mother, but that was merely conjecture as Caía didn't know. Unlike the impermanent layers of tape plastered over her own mailbox down the street, the name on Marta's box gave a clear indication that the house she lived in didn't often change hands—which only meant, to Caía, that the woman must have some money...

Was she the reason Nick had come to Spain?
What was his connection to that woman and her child?

All three resided here together. And though it was perfectly conceivable that he was renting space, as Caía was doing, she didn't think so. Why would anyone stir himself to escort some kid to school every day, unless he was invested? No, the task was too much for a mere tenant, even a saintly one, which Nick Kelly most assuredly was not.

You're not the world's police, Caía.
Whatever.
Women have to look out for one another, don't they?

The answer to that question was unequivocally "Yes."

Caía took another drag of the cigarette and her gut turned.

An image of Nick Kelly trolling around dating sites for unwary victims popped into her head. So, of course, that's what he'd done. Although... why would he abandon his life—a successful one by most standards—and come here to Spain to play nanny to a little girl?

It doesn't make sense.

Admittedly, none of the answers that came to mind suited Caía's narrative, save one. Unfortunately, as much as she hated the truth, he wasn't here to escape justice. Bottom line: To be criminally liable for her son's accident, the traffic homicide investigation would have had to prove that the driver had been reckless or criminally negligent—excessive speed, texting while driving, that sort of thing. From day one, Nick Kelly had been free to go wherever he pleased. But that didn't mean he was blameless. For fuck's sake, he ran over a kid—her kid.

How did someone get to walk away from something like that?

Caía inhaled another drag, and her throat seized. She peered down at the cigarette in her hand, and hurled it to the ground, grinding it into the sidewalk with the toe of her sandal.

She didn't even know how to smoke. It made her sick. For God's sake, she was at an all-time low. It was hard work hating someone full time, and it was taking a toll.

First, her mother. Then her son. Then her father. And if that wasn't enough, Gregg had left her when she'd needed him most, but fine. *Whatever.* There's your word again, Gregg. *I get it now. It feels good to say it.* Freeing. It was like divesting oneself of responsibility. *Whatever.*

They claimed divorce was difficult, but Caía's was easy. Her husband was there one day, the next he was gone. But unlike her son's, Gregg's absence was a relief.

For months and months after the accident, Caía had sat in her hospital room, staring out her window, hoping to see her son's face in the glass . . . and, of course, it was an impossibility.

Rather, what she saw, over and over, was her own reflection in the depths of that bathroom mirror, fine red cracks radiating from a center where her forehead had impacted with glass.

She lost herself in that memory for a moment, tasting nicotine in the back of her throat.

At some point, Gregg had discovered her there, standing in the upstairs bathroom—the one closest to Jack's room—her arms hanging limply at her sides, her blood draining onto the tile, staining the grout. Despair, black and ugly, had been simmering deep in her gut, like liquid hate boiling in a cauldron. She'd stood there, in that bathroom, looking into that mirror—so clean, not a speck of toothpaste anywhere on it—and fury rose up inside her, building to a terrifying climax... as it was doing again now.

Later, at the hospital, voices had filtered in from the hall. "Do you think she did it on purpose?"

To her husband's credit, there had been a bit of sorrow in his answer. "I don't know," he'd said. "I don't know."

And then a pause, followed by the same female voice. "Mr. Paine, let me rephrase the question. Do you believe your wife presents a danger to herself?"

For a long, long time, Gregg hadn't responded, and then he'd said, "Yes." And again, with much more certainty, "Yes."

And that was that.

Later, once they were alone, Dr. Hale explained, "Some degree of anger is normal, Caía. It's a natural part of the grieving process. Do you understand what I'm telling you?"

Caía's throat had felt too thick to speak. Something large was stationed there, swallowing words before they could form.

"Caía, are you listening to me?" There had been a note of impatience in the woman's voice, enough to keep Caía from answering. "Often, with disordered anger, episodes can be more intense." And more firmly, she asked, "Caía... do you understand what I'm saying?"

How the hell did they expect her to process so much? Losing her mom was difficult enough. But then her whole world had expired in the space of a year. Caía's mother gave up her fight against cancer the year before Jack's death. Afterward, her father went downhill fast. The two had been inseparable, and Jack's death was the final straw. Caía buried her son on June 18, 2016, and her dad on August 5, 2016—*whap, whap, whap*—rapid-fire heartbreak. And then Gregg dumped her and something snapped.

Whatever.

"Caía?"

Caía had blinked in answer, her throat suffocating her. Her shoulders had tensed until they were made of pain itself.

No one needed to explain to her why she was feeling what she was feeling. "My son is dead," she'd answered coldly.

Lowering her lashes, the doctor had peered down at the papers in her lap—documents that presumably declared Caía unfit to care for herself. "Yes, I know," she'd said.

I know.

I know. I know. I know.

Well, did she also know it was Jack's birthday the day he died? Did she know Caía had bought him a brand-new skateboard, along with another surprise?

Sleek and black with a white marbled moon, the skateboard had been one Jack had been eyeing online for weeks, but not even Caía knew what was inside the accompanying box. Whatever it held was worth more than twice what she'd paid for the skateboard. "Unknown treasures, all handpicked for the avid skateboarder," the description said.

Still, to this day, she didn't know what was inside that fucking box. His old skateboard had been crushed beneath the wheels of Nick Kelly's car, and after her son died, Caía had carried the unopened package to the Dumpster and taken an axe to the brand-new skateboard. And then she'd burned whatever remained in the fire pit in the backyard, wheels and all. She could still recall the smell of rubber, as distinct as the scent of her own blood.

Disordered anger, the doctor had explained, usually presented as a secondary symptom. It was not uncommon with grief, but since Caía had already harmed herself once, she would be better served to remain under expert supervision so they could help her "reconvene on a path to recovery"—reconvene, as though she were meeting someone on an actual path.

Really, what they were trying to say was this: Gregg didn't want to be responsible for Caía or her grief. Her husband was too busy to mourn their son. He had things to do, places to go, people to see. Girlfriends to screw.

Caía, on the other hand, had nothing better to do than to experience all five stages of grief. Really, there were five stages. But who were these clever people who'd presumed to sum up what was essentially an existential implosion of the soul, going so far as to give each stage discernible names that you could check off, like a to-do list?

In the end, none of those stages, except anger, had been relevant to Caía. She neither had the capacity to deny her son's death, nor had they allowed her the liberty to mourn him in peace. Even now, the absence of her duties as Jack's mother were excruciating.

Every time she didn't wake up to pack his lunch, or rush home to wash his soccer pants, she remembered. She also remembered every time she didn't have to clean his bathroom mirror...

Caía swallowed a ball of grief.

Across the street, the front door of Nº 5 Calle Lealas opened—a massive door surrounded by ornate baroque stonework. Just inside, beyond the foyer, was a second ironwork door, adding fortification. The only thing she'd ever glimpsed beyond those barriers was the soft glow of more salmon paint and the distant impression of a sunlit back door.

Out came a fiery-haired older woman, producing a set of keys. There was no knob on the outside, only a keyhole. She locked the door, then pushed the face of it before ambling away.

A housekeeper? Maybe a grandmother?

Caía thought perhaps she might be a housekeeper, because she preferred to think of those people as spoiled and privileged and a house that size was bound to employ servants. Although really, it was impossible to say how big the house could be.

Judging by its depth along the alley, not very small.

Out front grew a lovely maple, its ever-increasing circumference buckling the sidewalk around its base—nature's dogged and subversive threat to civil order.

Without constant care, people and places buckled to their nature. It couldn't only be Caía who waged a perpetual war with her demons.

Proof of this came marching past as Caía stood waiting for the super mercado to open its doors. It came in the form of a drunken brunette, with thick black eye makeup that no longer complemented her Spanish eyes. Water soluble, the liner had smeared into dark streaks that stained her cheek bones, wearing into well-earned wrinkles. Heels off, brandishing them like weapons, the woman screamed at the top of her lungs, "¡Hijo de puta!" *Son of a whore.* "¡Asqueroso!" *Disgusting man.* "¡Boracho!" *Drunk.* And on and on she went, marching past, continuing her tirade, her voice echoing perversely down empty streets.

Later, she would pull herself together.
Maybe.

Nº 5 Calle Lealas sat on a quiet corner. The super mercado occupied the space across the street, and directly opposite the house, on the southeast corner, sat a lovely church. Iglesia de la Victoria, the plaque read. A single turret overlooked the street—as though watching over the house—an ancient tower, with a blue-and-white tiled dome. Caía wasn't the least bit religious anymore, but guilt and shame had no denomination.

In her periphery, she spied movement inside the market. Feeling sick to her stomach, she stood another moment, staring at the door across the street, and then peered after the shouting woman, feeling lost. How much further must she fall before she ended up like that?

Maybe you've gone too far already?

The woman in the market unlocked the door, shoving it open to allow Caía entry. But Caía didn't go inside. She didn't even have a damned coffeemaker. Pretending suddenly felt unhinged. She smiled wanly at the women, and shook her head, then walked away.

Three

If you gaze long enough into an abyss,
the abyss will gaze back into you.
— *Friedrich Nietzsche*

CHICAGO, FRIDAY, JUNE 10, 2016
NICK

LIKE THE UPPERCUT JAB OF A RANK FIST, THE SCENT OF URINE PLOWED UP INTO NICK'S NOSTRILS. Most days, it was the wafting odor of fair-trade coffee he focused on. Today, gray skies, surly faces, and an ass-chapping wind did nothing to ease the scent of fermenting urine in Chicago's former meat-packing district. This was the city's final urban frontier, home to trending art galleries, tasting rooms, and up-and-coming wealth management agencies. Hey, if it was good enough for Google, it should be good enough for Starr Wealth Management. On his way into the building, outside the Starr parking garage, a woman stepped into Nick's path. "L fare?" she begged.

With dirty blond hair and bruised skin, she might have been pretty except for the scabs all over her face. She held a palm out. That was the thing about industrial grit, it came with a bit more reality than some folks were prepared to accept.

Automatically, Nick reached into his pocket. But he stopped short as he focused on the tremor of her hand. The scabs were indicative of a meth user. Her sleeves were rolled down in eighty-degree weather. She shivered as she stared up at him. Roughly twenty. He wasn't doing her any favors by paying for another fix. "Sorry," he said, fingering the silver in his pocket. "I got nothing." And still some part of him itched to lift out the coins and sprinkle them into her hand.

For an awkward moment, he waffled, and her eyes snapped to his brand-new suit, then to his briefcase, returning to his face, the look in her eyes scathing. "Fuck off," she said hatefully, her face twisting with what could only be described as a deep-seated loathing. Nick shook his head, brushing past her. "Think you're better'n me?" she screamed. "Fuck yourself, mother-fuckin' coal cracker!" Nick was Irish, but he'd never seen the inside of a coal mine. In fact, neither had his father or his grandfather. But some hatreds ran deep, like that piss scent that couldn't be eradicated with a little bit of North Side toilet water.

His shoulders tensed as he walked away, his grip tightening on his briefcase. *You can't save the world*, he told himself, but his thoughts returned to the phone conversation with Marta. Without distraction for the remainder of the way into the office, he thought about his brother's wife.

Inside the Starr building, all throughout the lobby, on the way up the elevator, he refrained from making eye contact, and he made it into his office without having to speak another sound.

Although she was normally in her chair long before Nick arrived, Amy wasn't in yet. He meant to speak to her this morning, figure out how to best handle their work relationship. Prying his white-knuckled grip from the handle, he sat the briefcase down on the chair facing his desk, unwilling to tackle the contents until he downed a shot of caffeine. He stretched his fingers and studied the indentations in his hand, shaking his head over the persistent tension. Coffee wasn't the answer, but he couldn't start his morning without it.

He'd never once asked Amy to fetch him a cup, but she usually rushed out after greeting him. Today, the office was quiet, none of the cubicles occupied yet, so he made a beeline into the kitchen. Once there, he fumbled with the coffeemaker, trying to figure out where to stick the cup. The damned things were like bathroom faucets; every one worked a little differently. Pushing and shoving and pressing, he nevertheless figured it out, and then he waited less than patiently for his cup to fill, all the while listening for sounds of life beyond the kitchen door. More than usual, he wasn't in the mood for idle chatter.

His luck held out. But the instant he walked into his office, the overhead lights flickered on. With the steaming cup in hand, Nick sank into his chair. And, for a long, disordered moment, he sat, staring at his briefcase, sipping from his coffee.

Clack. Clack. Clack.

Not heels. Hard leather. Long purposeful strides. The footfalls grew louder and louder, going on and on for the length of the office—half the size of a football field—all the way back to Nick's office. He'd left the door open for Amy, but it was Sam Starr who knocked on the doorframe. "Morning," he said.

Nick gave his boss—and friend—a half-hearted smile. "Did you come all this way to give me a morning kiss, or something else on your mind?"

Sam shuffled in, moving Nick's briefcase from the chair and setting it aside to replace it with his Prada-covered ass. He flicked a perfectly manicured fingernail over his graying sideburns—proof that, if you had any conscience, this business waged war with your physical being. "Quick on the draw, straight to the point, that's what I like best about you, Nick."

Nick took a sip of his coffee. "Yeah?"

The senior partner of his firm sank into the chair facing him, crossing his legs. "It's Amy," Sam said.

Nick nodded, half expecting it to be the case. "Did she come talk to you this morning?"

"No, yesterday, but not for any reason you might think. She told me everything, Nick."

The tension in Nick's shoulders returned. "Told you what?"

"About Jimmy."

"Oh," he said, and his head fell back against the headrest of his chair. Beneath his breath, he said, "Damn it."

"You can't fire her for telling us. Fact is, you shouldn't be sharing pillow-talk with her at all." Sam was one to talk. On the other hand, Nick had never allowed himself to get involved with an employee before now, despite the office being about as incestuous as they came. Shared happy hours made it too easy to slip into a coworker's bed. Except it wasn't like that for Nick. He normally kept his pants tightly zipped. Amy had been a willing shoulder in a weak moment.

Still, it was no excuse. Nick was her boss. He sat his coffee cup down on the desk, leaning forward, lifting a hand to his temple. "So, you'll give her a new assignment?"

Sam allowed him a moment to play out all the possible consequences—his card-carrying right as the "Starr" partner of the firm. Except that Nick outdid him nine months out of twelve. That, more than the fact that he and Sam had once shared a college dorm, was Nick's assurance that his "consequences" would amount to something less than a slap on the wrist. He was far more concerned about Amy than he was about himself. "She needs the job," Nick said.

"Don't worry about it; we'll work it out."

"Good."

Out in the general assembly room, the morning influx of employees had already begun. Sounds of light switches clicking on, telephone receivers being lifted, and buttons being punched increased, but in Nick's office, the silence was absolute. After a long, uncomfortable moment, Sam said, "Is there anything we can do?"

"No."

"If you need time off, you'll let me know?"

"It's not going to affect my bottom line."

Sam nodded. He grabbed his jaw, massaging it hard, a nervous tell that Nick recognized all too well. There was something else Sam wanted to say, but he'd already talked himself out of it.

"I'll be sure to keep you posted," Nick said.

"All righty." Sam stood and turned to go. "Tell Jimmy he's in our thoughts."

*

JERÉZ, PRESENT DAY

Like a zombie, Caía wandered in and out of shops.

Moments of clarity had begun to creep in, like intrepid little beings in a brave new world. This morning was the first time she'd missed watching Nick walk his charge to school, and now she was leaning toward skipping the café altogether.

Somehow, being here, breaking old habits, had already begun to erode Caía's resolve. But that wasn't all. Along with a bit of clarity came a sour dose of reality.

Maybe, just maybe, after all, she had learned something during her thirty-six weeks of anger management intervention—even if her most positive results were only now making themselves known.

It was entirely possible she'd simply needed to see him. Or maybe she was drawn to Nick Kelly for reasons she hadn't yet determined. Certainly, Caía wasn't anyone's judge or jury.

Neither was she anyone's executioner. She didn't even believe in the death penalty. She was just a crazy mother who couldn't let go of her sun—and no, that wasn't a misnomer. Jack was her sun. Her little boy had been the center of her universe.

"Happiness can only exist in acceptance," her therapist had said, in that decisive and Zen-like tone reserved for yoga instructors, AA sponsors, and mental health specialists.

Well, screw that. Acceptance was something Caía never meant to embrace. Accept the inevitability of her son's death? *No way.*

On the other hand, she accepted these things: She would never again get to tousle Jack's hair; she would never experience the joy of watching him grow into a man; she would never get to meet his first date . . . *Was he the sort of guy who liked to dance? Would he have been a great husband and dad? Would he have become an architect some day? An engineer?*

No matter what you gave him, or how much it cost, Jack liked to disassemble things, figure out what made them tick, and put them back together again. Unfortunately, some things couldn't be returned to working order.

Like you, Jack.

Unjustly, she'd been deprived of the rest of her son's story. His life was a ravaged book, full of pages brutally wrenched out, leaving only tattered glimpses of what might have been . . . half a word here and there, staring out from behind decimated pages.

Mulling over the past year of her life, the changes she had made—leaving Chicago so abruptly—Caía tried to imagine what should come next, after this . . . whatever this was.

Unanchored by meaningful relationships, the future presented itself as a blank page—as blank as the pages of her son's life book.

Nick Kelly was only a man—not even all that frightening, if the truth be known. He looked inherently sad, smiling only when he addressed that little girl. *Was it possible Jack's death had devastated him as well? Had he come here to escape himself?*

Mulling over these questions, and more, she ducked into a small artisan shop where flamenco figurines teetered precariously at the edges of shelves. Some wore long, flowing polka-dotted skirts painted red and white. But more than the flamenco dolls, Caía loved the hand-painted fans.

The shop owner, a leathery-skinned man dressed all in black with a sapphire-blue scarf tied about his neck, hurried over, pointing to a gold-leaf signature below the plaits of the black fan she held in her hand. "Mira," he said. *Look.* "Éste . . ." He tapped his finger on the sticks and guards. "De sándalo," he said emphatically. "Tajada a mano." He enunciated the words clearly, as though he'd already pegged Caía for a tourist.

Carved from sandalwood, the fan was signed by the artist, which might or might not have been the shop owner for all the pride registered on his face. He seized the fan from Caía's hand and flicked it open with the grace and speed a South Side gangster might have used to brandish a knife. But instead of stabbing her with it, he merely fanned himself, stomping his feet like a flamenco dancer and batting his lashes like a virgin. Then, he returned the fan to Caía.

He cut a dashing, if slightly clichéd figure—a Gitano wearing a bolero jacket and heels that went *clack, clack*. And maybe he was flirting a little bit, as well. Although Caía wasn't the least bit attracted to him. Still, the effort made her smile.

She ran a finger along the slightly raised edges of the signature. "Muy bonito," she said, and the man rewarded her with a genuine smile. Mimicking the same fluid motion of his hand, Caía spread the fan's plaited leafs to reveal pink roses painted on stained black wood. She brought the fan to her face, covering her smile, and fanning herself coyly before pausing to peek over the frilly edge. Imitating the shopkeeper, she batted her lashes playfully.

"¡Olé, olé!" the shopkeeper said, and clapped his hands. Caía smiled. This time it wasn't fake. In fact, for the first time since her son's death, her lips curved of their own accord. So, of course, she bought the fan.

Feeling lighter than she had in years, she thanked the shopkeeper, moving out of his shop and into the street, inhaling the citrusy scent of sunshine . . . and bread. She made her way across the street to the panadería to grab a fresh baguette.

Her appetite still hadn't returned, but she meant to tempt herself, hoping to recapture that *joie de vivre* she'd once had. It used to be that everything was a new adventure for Caía. Sushi. Zumba. Kayaking. Now, nothing held much appeal. The gazpacho yesterday had tasted bland, the little grains of spices like bits of glass against her tongue.

Inside the panadería, the afternoon sun glinted off the edges of the counters. A short line of customers had already formed, waiting for their turns. By this hour of the day, the shops were all preparing to close for the afternoon, drawing in last-minute shoppers, and judging by the line, this bread was quite the thing.

Drawn by the scents that escaped into the street after Caía opened the door, a few more people filtered in after her, until the shop was full and they were packed like sardines in a can. But for once, Caía didn't mind. Content to stand and wait her turn, she shifted to make room, her nostrils flaring over the odors that accosted her here—warm stones and years and years of baked crust on the insides of the ovens, toasted butter, maybe a bit of sugar. All these were scents that reminded her of her mom. Recipes handed down by her grandmother—a woman she'd never met but wished she had. And yet, despite the tantalizing scents, there was no adrenaline rush, no thrill of anticipation—not until the woman at the front of the line turned and Caía saw her face. Like an old car battery with jumper cables attached, Caía's heart gave a little start.

For the smallest fraction of an instant, their eyes met and held. Caía searched for recognition, but there was none. Taking her bread purchase with her, the woman smiled as she made her way back through the crowd, out the door, turning slightly as she slid past Caía, forced to look away as she edged her way past waiting customers, into the amber-lit street. Ignoring the little voice inside that said, "Don't do it." Caía fell out of line and followed.

Four

I measure every grief I meet with narrow, probing eyes – I wonder if it weighs like mine – or has an easier size.
– *Emily Dickinson*

STOP. *Slip inside a shop, Caía. Any shop. Distract yourself.*
The stubborn clip of her own heels along the cobbled sidewalk made Caía physically ill. Wholly unaware that Caía was pursuing her, Marta Herrera Nuñez stopped to chat with a woman outside a shop. Caía held back, pretending to read a sidewalk menu.

Jamón ibérico. Papas bravas. Pimientos fritos.

She could never remember which was which: pimiento or pimienta. If the ones on this menu were fried, they must be the vegetable. It figured they would make the spicy stuff feminine. She rolled her eyes. She had been in Jeréz now for weeks and had yet to try any of the traditional dishes gracing nearly every tapas menu in the city. Occasionally, if she ordered a glass of wine, they surprised her with a dish, laying it down beside her beverage, but she had very little desire to celebrate this trip with food. Sorrow and guilt—yes, guilt—turned everything rancid in her mouth. However, guilt was a facet of her grief she didn't dare explore—not yet. Like a moth trapped inside her head, something vile fluttered at the edges of her consciousness, something Caía didn't want to think about . . .

The woman Marta was speaking with nodded, then disappeared into her shop. She returned momentarily with a small brown sack, which she then handed to Marta. The two exchanged kisses, and Marta resumed her stroll down the street. Once again, Caía fell in behind her.

So, is this what you've become? A stalker?

That was one more thing to blame Nick Kelly for, because Caía was not behaving like herself. A sudden, inescapable burst of anger threatened her composure, immediately unseating her morning's buoyancy. *Why? Why are you doing this? Why? Why? Why?*

Just like that time in Caía's fourth-grade class, she feared she would melt to the ground and lay sobbing over the unfairness of it all. But she didn't. She kept walking, her gaze shifting from the lovely cobbled patterns on the ancient sidewalk to the woman who remained oblivious to her pursuit. A citrusy perfume wafted on the air. Row upon row of orange trees lined the city streets, rich with green foliage and low-lying fruit. No one paid the oranges any mind. Within reach, it would be easy to pluck one as she passed. Like the petite brunette walking ahead of her, the temptation was too much to bear.

Of course, Caía had nothing against Marta. If anything, she felt sorry for the woman. And, really, the only danger she was in was for Caía to shake her hard enough to rattle sense into her head. *What, in God's name, are you doing with that man?*

Poor, poor Marta. She seemed so vulnerable walking with her shopping basket in hand and that long, long baguette tucked beneath one arm. She didn't even realize Caía had followed her into the city mercado, and once inside, Caía's self-recrimination intensified.

You really are a stalker, she told herself.

Happy, Caía? Get a grip. Go home.

It was nearly 2:00 p.m. now. The stalls were closing, but if you followed the scent of fish into the heart of the mercado, there were no empty stalls here, not yet. It was easy to imagine why: Fish stayed fresh for only so long. Of course, the fishmongers would wish to sell their catches as quickly as possible. Caía felt that same sense of urgency as she watched Marta stop to examine a display of fish on ice. Organized in neat little rows, with heads and tails intact and mouths agape, a multitude of tiny black eyes winked at passersby. She hovered close enough to eavesdrop. "Where is your brother?" Marta asked, in Spanish.

"No está aquí," the vendor replied, and Marta muttered something cross beneath her breath, peering about. With a sigh, she turned back to the fishmonger, clearly frustrated to be dealing with him instead of the brother.

"¿Hay atún?"

Sober-faced, holding a wicked-looking blade at his side, the fishmonger scowled at Marta, evidently no more pleased to be dealing with her as she was with him. "Claro," he said.

"¿Pero fresco?"

"Mujer, ¿no tienes ojos en la cara?"

"Sí, Jose Luis, pero también tengo nariz." Marta tapped at the side of her nose, and the two launched into a heated discourse that, to the best of Caía's understanding, was a clear indication that their feud was not new. Marta impugned the freshness of his fish, he told her to shop somewhere else, she said she would tell his brother, and he invited her to leave—not so politely.

Caía hid her smile behind her hand as the fishmonger dismissed Marta with a wave of his hand. "Vete a la mierda," the man said, and Marta drew her baguette like a sword.

"Hijo de puta," she countered, and Caía blushed over their interaction—insults delivered so easily. And yet it seemed that none of their discourse was unexpected or unusual, and he moved on to the next person in his line with aplomb, a young mother, bouncing a toddler on her hip.

As passionately as the two had spoken, the battle was immediately forgotten, and Caía marveled at it ending so easily. They'd spoken their minds and held nothing back. The woman next in line didn't even acknowledge the argument and smiled as she asked Jose Luis for bacalao.

There was something about the way the mother's arm curled so possessively about her child that gave Caía a pang of grief. For an instant, she sensed a phantom weight on her own hip, a sensation that was immediately ripped away, and her throat thickened at the renewed sense of loss.

It took her a moment to recover, and then her eyes once again sought Marta.

With the vendor forgotten, Marta had moved on to the next stall, examining almejas and mejillones. The mollusks were shut tight, prepared for a fight. Suddenly Marta turned to look at Caía, her brows twitching slightly.

Half out of embarrassment, half out of nervousness, Caía blurted in Spanish, "Perdóname, señora. ¿Recomiendas el pesado?"

Marta furrowed her brow. "¿Qué?"

Wholly uncomfortable now, Caía gave a nod toward the fishmonger, who was bartering with his new customer, to far better results. The young mom nodded enthusiastically, smiling as Jose Luis plucked up a piece of fish to gut while she watched.

"Ah, yes," Marta said, with sudden understanding. "Eres Americana, ¿no?"

"Sí."

Marta's doleful eyes crinkled at the corners, managing to look both happy and sad at the same time. She peered over at the fishmonger, and back. "He is stubborn. But you say pesado, and I think you mean pescado, ¿verdad?" When Caía managed to look confused, Marta reshuffled the items in her hands and persevered to explain, "You say to me, 'recomiendas el pesado?' and this means, 'you recommend the stubborn.' But I think you have meant the fish, not the man, yes?"

The difference of a single letter.

Heat rose into Caía's cheeks. "Yes," she said. "I did mean the fish. My Spanish is rusty, I'm sorry," she said.

Marta smiled. "No, it is good."

"Gracias."

"And his fish is also good," Marta said. "But his attitude is how you say? Atrocious. I do not know how his brother leaves him to deal with customers. Men are infuriating, are they not?"

Caía smiled. "They certainly can be." But infuriating was the least libelous thing she had to say about Nick Kelly. Only now that she had Marta's full attention, his name refused to come to her lips. She felt tongue-tied and shy, uncertain what to say next. In fact, for the first time since her son's accident, Caía dared to consider the unthinkable possibility of Nick Kelly's innocence. What if she spoke out of turn? She might ruin his life. As he'd ruined hers.

Thank the woman and walk away.

Some strange moral imperative kept Caía's feet rooted to the spot and her mouth shut. She couldn't prove Nick's culpability, but she felt obligated to protect Marta and her daughter.

Besides, there was something about Marta Herrera Nuñez that made Caía long to rush into her arms . . . and cry. "Your English is very good," Caía offered.

Marta smiled. "Me casé con un Americano." *She'd married an American.* "My husband is from Chicago," she offered in English, with nearly perfect diction, and then she proceeded to unfold her shopping basket to prepare it for its burden. Uncertain what more to say, Caía watched her, reluctant to leave. She was grateful when Marta asked, "You have been to this city?"

"Chicago?"

"Sí."

"Well . . . I suppose, most people pass through at some point. It's a big city."

Marta turned her full attention on Caía then, her chocolate-brown eyes inviting Caía to spill her guts. It would have been so easy for her to brush Caía off and continue with her shopping, but everything about Marta, from her body language to the directness of her gaze, invited Caía to linger.

"Yes? And what about you?"

Caía shrugged, looking away. "Well, yes . . . I did live . . . there . . . for a while . . . my son . . ." She peered down at her feet. "He died."

Marta's fingers lifted to her lips. Her eyes slanted sadly, and for an instant Caía feared she would burst into tears.

"I am so sad to hear this," Marta said, and a familiar knot rose in her throat. It had been months now since she had spoken so openly about Jack's death, and she swallowed the emotions that rose to choke her breath away.

Marta's eyes locked with hers, intensely expressive. "I'm so sorry. No mother should outlive her children," she said. "It is a terrible thing to lose a husband, and more terrible yet to lose a child. What is your son's name?"

Is, she'd said. *Is*.

Marta's English was exceptional, although tenses were notoriously difficult. Even so, Caía was comforted by the present tense of her question, even realizing it must be a mistake. Wholly grateful for the opportunity to speak about Jack in the present, she said, "Jack."

"In my language, I think it is Joaquín."

"Joaquín?" Caía said, testing the name. She liked the sound of it.

"Yes, I believe so."

Together, they drifted away from the vendor, neither quite prepared to end the conversation, and for a long interval the two women stood staring at one another, awkwardly, though familiar in a way Caía couldn't explain. Whatever it was she'd been searching for when she'd set out to follow Marta, this wasn't it, but this was something—something Caía hadn't realized she'd needed so badly until this moment, faced with the undiluted empathy of a stranger.

Silence stretched between them, but it wasn't entirely uncomfortable. They shared a strange communion in the middle of that mercado, with people rushing past.

"Someday, I would love to take my Laura to Chicago," Marta said.

Laura.

That must be the name of the little girl Nick Kelly walked to school every day. Inexplicably, Caía felt a fierce and inescapable protectiveness over both mother and daughter.

As she stood there, Marta dropped her baguette and Caía reached for it, catching it before it hit the dirty floor. "Here, let me help." She slid the bread beneath her own arm, reaching out again to take more of the burden from Marta's hands, leaving Marta's hands free to hold her shopping basket. "It's heavy," Caía said, surprised by the weight of the brown sack.

Marta smiled again. "Aceite de oliva," she explained. "My friend María orders the best of the best from Baena and tonight I will make a paella for my Laura's fiesta de cumpleaños."

"Oh. Well . . . then I should buy some," Caía said. She shouldn't feel such an affinity with this woman, but she did. "One can never have enough olive oil, I say."

"Well, yes, I agree. Please, you must allow me to thank you properly. María's shop is very close by." She reached out to grasp Caía's arm, squeezing gently. "Only wait for me," she commanded, and then returned to the vendor, ordering two dozen mejillones. Smiling, the woman placed Marta's mussels into a bag, tied off the bag, and handed it to Marta. Marta placed the mussels into her basket. "¿Cuánto es?" she asked the woman behind the counter.

"Doce," the vendor said, and Marta produced a stack of bills from the front pocket of her jeans, counting out twelve euros and handing them over to the woman. The woman thanked Marta, and Marta turned to Caía, looping an arm about hers in a familiar way, "Venga," she demanded, "follow me. It is the best I may do for my new amiga from Chicago."

And that was that.

Open and forthcoming, Marta chatted on and on about her love for the city in which she'd been born. Jeréz, she explained—shifting easily from Spanish to English and then back again, and sometimes using both in the same sentence—was a wonderful place to live.

Was Caía thinking of moving here? How exciting! Barrio Santiago was the most renowned flamenco neighborhood "en todo el mundo." And, of course, it was the sherry capital of the world, which was to say, if it wasn't made in Jeréz, it wasn't sherry. And by the by, her friends owned a bodega in the city; maybe Caía had been there already? And if not, she would love to take her. As far as olive oil was concerned, simply no oil was better than the aceite produced in Baena, a very tiny village in the Provence of Córdoba, very close to the river Marbella. "Un pueblecito muy bonito," Marta said. Although she had never been anywhere besides Andalusia, she didn't have to leave Andalusia to know good olive oil. "Tell me, Caía, have you visited the Plaza de España in Sevilla?" she asked, without segue. "If not, you must go at once. This is where I met my husband and his brother. Nico is a such a good man," she said. "I would love for you to meet him."

Nico, she'd said. *Nick*. And hearing his name, it took Caía a dizzying moment to respond. "Yes, I'm sure he is." She tasted bile in the back of her throat. "I would . . . love . . . to meet him."

"Truly?"

"Yes, why not?"

"¡Maravilloso!" Marta exclaimed. "You are both from Chicago. How strange is the world we live in. Yes?"

"Yes," Caía agreed. "Quite strange."

Acutely aware of the arm looped about hers, they made their way down the street, chatting endlessly—or rather, Marta chatted on and on, none the wiser that Caía knew precisely where she'd procured her oil. They passed the shop, and Caía stiffened as they walked by without stopping.

Marta was so immersed in their conversation—thrilled over the prospect of Caía meeting her "Nico"—that it never occurred to her that the familiarity of their stroll might give Caía reason for discomfort. Why should it? They passed by other women on the street, walking arm in arm, even holding hands. Caía longed to pull away, but some part of her clung gratefully to the gesture of friendship. Even Lucy had distanced herself from Caía, unwilling to hear Caía's endless ruminations about Jack—even less willing to hear that Caía held Nick Kelly responsible for his death. The day Caía told her she was coming to Spain was the last time they'd spoken.

"Caía, why can't you let it go?" Lucy had asked, and Caía's anger was explosive.

"Let what go, Lucy? My son?! I don't have a choice, do I? He's gone and that son of a bitch is to blame."

The deep, unbearable silence that followed eroded years of friendship. And then Lucy said, "No good will come of it, Caía."

But Lucy couldn't possibly understand. She and her husband had never even wanted children. This had always been a point of contention between them, because Lucy felt judged, believing wrongly that Caía thought less of her because she didn't long to change diapers. Except it wasn't true. "I have to go," she'd said, and she'd meant to Spain, but Lucy took it as an out.

"Yeah, me too. I've got things to do."

"What things?" Caía had wanted to ask, but she didn't. They'd hung up the phone, and that was the last conversation they ever had.

Inexplicably, Marta made Caía feel comfortable in a way she hadn't known with Lucy since the day Jack was born.

As they made their way down the cobbled street, surrounded by elaborate buildings that were older than any Caía had ever seen, Caía learned Marta was the great, great granddaughter of an ambassador to Portugal. It was her great, great grandfather who'd built the house on Calle Lealas. But the family lost it during Franco's rule. Her father reacquired it during the eighties and left it to Marta when he passed. Listening for the most part, Caía drank in the wealth of information Marta seemed so eager to oblige her with. Many of her questions were answered with Caía never having to utter a word. But it wasn't only Marta spilling her guts. The urge to confess herself was strong, and Caía found herself telling Marta about her divorce and the bitter disappointment she'd felt when Gregg turned out to be such a fair-weather husband.

"So, divorce is what brings you to Spain?"

Caía inhaled sharply and slowly let it out. "Partly."

"Well, my friend, Jeréz will treat you very well. How long will you stay?"

Caía inhaled once more. "I'm not sure."

And then, suddenly, Marta stopped walking and stamped her foot. "Coño," she said emphatically. "I forgot to take you to María's shop. You see how I do not remember from one minute to the next?" She placed a hand to her temple and twisted a finger, making the universal sign for crazy, but if this was crazy, then what Caía was doing was certifiably insane.

Nevertheless, Caía too had been so lost in their conversation that even she hadn't realized where they stood—outside the super mercado across the street from the house.

"Bueno, mañana," Marta said, and once again, she reached out to squeeze Caía's arm. "Tonight, you must come to my house for paella. I will introduce you to Laura and to Nico. Sí?"

Startled by the invitation, Caía's mouth parted to speak, but no words emerged.

Mistaking her reaction, Marta insisted, "Yes, my dear, you must. There will be plenty to eat, and my daughter will love to practice her English with you. Please say yes."

"Okay," Caía said, fighting the overwhelming desire to look over at the house across the street, to see if a disturbingly familiar face was looking out from the upstairs balcony.

Completely unaware of her inner turmoil, Marta's face split into a wide grin. Her eyes twinkled like black diamonds. "Bueno, chica, aqui está mi casa," she said, lifting her chin and inclining her head in the direction of Nº 5 Calle Lealas. "Dinner is served tonight at eight, but you are welcome to join us now for a glass of sherry."

"Now?"

She nodded once, emphatically. "Claro."

Something like fire ants crawled into the pit of Caía's gut. "Well, no . . . I can't—" She shook her head. "Not now, but I will see you tonight . . . at eight? I have more shopping . . . to do."

Marta thumped a hand against her forehead. "Ah, yes. Yes, of course," she said. "Because I have taken you away from the mercado before you could finish. I am sorry, Caía, but then you must arrive at eight, sí?"

"Yes," Caía said, forcing a smile.

Marta's hand embraced her arm once again, only this time with a bit more force. "Que bien. I will eagerly anticipate you." And then, she kissed Caía once on each cheek, the way she'd done with her friend from the olive oil shop. She turned away, and Caía kept her gaze trained on Marta's back, waving when she waved, never once looking up at the balcony above her front door, where the figure of a man stood beside a little girl.

Caía heard their voices as she turned away, rapid-fire words from Marta, and the soft, calm tenor of a man's response. A happy child. The familial sounds squeezed at Caía's heart. Only now, at long last, she would have the chance to face the man who killed her son.

Mission accomplished, right?

So why did she feel so terrified?

Talk to me, Jack. Do you think I'm nuts?

Sensing three pairs of eyes on her back, Caía hurried away before Marta could call her back.

༄

CHICAGO, MONDAY, JUNE 13, 2016
CAÍA

"What are you doing?"

"Homework."

"It doesn't look like homework to me," Caía told her son as she peered over his shoulder at the computer screen, only to verify that what she glimpsed on her iPad was true. He was ogling that skateboard again, the one with the marbled moon. Caía had already bought it for him for his birthday, along with an accompanying surprise box, but he couldn't know that. His twelve-year-old brain—soon to be thirteen—couldn't put two and two together. She could see everything he was doing. Because their computers were connected under Caía's account, clicking that little icon on her finder took her straight to whatever Jack was looking at on his browser in the bedroom. That's how she'd determined which skateboard to buy him for his birthday. However, his grades were down, so maybe the computer shouldn't live in his room if he couldn't stay focused. "Get up," she demanded.

He looked shell-shocked by the command. "Ma?"

"Get up, Jack. We're moving your computer."

"Where?"

"Into the kitchen."

"Ma," he complained. "I'm not done with my homework yet."

"I don't care. Let's go. Up," Caía demanded.

"Mom!"

"I'm not going to argue with you, Jack. We're moving this computer into the kitchen, where I can watch you work while I cook."

"Why?"

"Because I said so." It wasn't the most reasonable answer, but if Jack hadn't yet figured out how she'd busted him, she wasn't going to give herself up now. He was still seated, looking at Caía with a wide-open mouth, as though he meant to argue but had thought better of it.

Caía was grateful he hadn't crossed that line yet, but she knew it was coming. She could sense it in his attitude, which was only getting worse and worse by the day. It could be his age, or it could be her husband's influence, in which case, she would be even more furious with Gregg for turning her son against her.

But maybe he wasn't doing it on purpose. Gregg was content enough to play the good cop, leaving Caía to do all the disciplining. He was an absent father, an absent husband, and God only knew, Caía had had enough. She swept in, unplugging the computer without turning it off.

"Dad says you're not supposed to do that," Jack said, his pubescent voice breaking slightly. "You'll break it. You're supposed to turn it off first, before you unplug it."

"I don't care what your father says."

Jack leapt up from his chair, moving out of her way, hands out as though Caía meant to frisk him. "It's not fair," he said melodramatically.

"What's not fair is that you don't seem capable of following rules. Now move," she said, kicking his chair so it rolled out of her way. She lifted the computer to carry it away. "Bring the keyboard."

"Mom!" he shouted behind her as she carted the screen out of his room. "I don't want to be in the kitchen."

"Too bad. You should have thought of that before."

"Before what? I was doing my homework," he whined.

"Yeah, I saw that." Never mind that she'd found the sync useful in ferreting out his birthday present. She wondered idly if he would figure out how she'd known once he opened his presents day after tomorrow. Would she tell him then? *Probably not.* Sooner or later, he'd figure it out on his own.

"You say you trust me but you don't."

Caía ignored the barb. "Trust is earned," she said, as she carted the computer into the kitchen and set it on the counter. She began to clean off the small desk area she had delegated for her cookbooks.

His father wasn't trustworthy, that was for sure. Caía would be damned if she'd allow her son to turn out the same way. She couldn't prove Gregg was cheating—again—but her gut said he was. Why else would he spend so much time at the gym? That day they'd run into the trainer at the Village

Tap—what was her name? Lindsey—she was nervous, avoiding eye-contact, except with Gregg. Down in her gut, Caía knew what that meant. Of course, Gregg had denied it, but Caía had finally understood why he had taken a sudden interest in his pecs. She literally couldn't count the number of times he'd flexed his muscles in the mirror before going to work. It was so cliché. He couldn't even cheat in a new and imaginative way.

For a long time, Jack didn't appear. She counted to ten, then twenty, hoping he would do as he was told and bring her the keyboard. If she had to go in after it, she was going to ground him, and she didn't want to do that two days before his birthday. Fortunately, as she removed the last cookbook from the countertop, Jack came in. He slammed the keyboard down on the counter, next to the computer. The crack of plastic and metal against the granite counter made her wince.

"It's not fair," he said again. "Dad's right. You're—"

Caía spun around, both hands going to her hips. "I am what?" she asked, going very still. If he dared utter that word his father used, she was going to lose her head.

"Never mind," Jack said, and he stomped away, toward the living room.

"No! Go to your room," Caía demanded.

He skidded to a halt and turned in the other direction, toward his room. "Why can't you be like Dad?" he asked from the hall, and Caía's face warmed. She heard his door slam and closed her eyes, inhaling a breath.

Why couldn't she be like his dad? Oh, boy. Why couldn't she be more like his dad?

Her face was as hot as a coal as she willed herself to calmly turn around. She hoisted up the computer from the counter and swung it over to the kitchen desk. Then she picked up and inspected the keyboard. Finding it still intact, she set it down beside the computer and turned the computer on, tapping the keys to make sure it wasn't broken.

As thin and fragile as it appeared, it was clearly more durable than she would have supposed. *Like Caía, perhaps. Like Jack.* Whatever happened, they would get through this. One way or the other, they would be fine. Caía would make sure of it. Leaning back on the counter, she thought about Jack at two, with his chubby little arms outstretched, and longed for simpler times. The memory launched her off the counter, toward his room.

The computer would have to stay in the kitchen, but her son probably needed a hug as badly as she did. Barefoot, she padded back to his room and knocked on his door.

"Jack," she said. He didn't answer, and Caía turned the knob.

He was seated at his empty desk with his old skateboard in hand, sour faced and angry, furiously spinning the skateboard's wheels. As dejected as he appeared right now, in but a few days, he would be grinning broadly at the sight of his brand-new skateboard. Right now, it was hidden beneath her bed, all wrapped up and ready to be unveiled. His dad, on the other hand, probably hadn't bothered to shop for anything at all, not even a card. He would pretend he'd been a part of Caía's gift planning, and Caía would allow it, because she wouldn't want to disappoint her son. She smiled. "How about we go for pizza tonight? I don't feel like cooking, after all."

Jack shrugged, but she could tell the prospect piqued his interest by the sideways glance he gave her. "What about Dad?"

"Dad won't be home until late; he can fend for himself."
Jack shrugged again. "I still have homework."
"I'll help you when we get home."
"I don't need any help, Mom."

Caía entered Jack's room and placed a hand on her son's shoulder. "Even better. We'll get home in time for you to finish, and I'll go read a book."

"Right," he said, shrugging, though not enough to dislodge her hand. "And then you'll hang out in the kitchen and spy on me?"

"Have you got something to hide, Jack?"

"No."

"Well, then nope—so, how about a truce?"

Reluctantly, Jack nodded. "Okay," he said, placing one arm around her waist, with the skateboard still hanging from his fingers. "Can we go to that place on North Clark Street—the one with the pizza pie in bowls?" His voice cracked and Caía pulled him closer, hugging him tight, inhaling the familiar scent of his hair. How much better could life get than sitting with your son across a table and eating pizza pot pie? No matter what, she couldn't regret a thing. Marrying Gregg had brought her this—this child. Her pride and joy. The true love of her life.

"Yep," she said.

"I need a new skateboard," he said, extricating himself and setting the beat-up old board down on the floor beneath his desk. "My wheels are wonky."

"We'll see what we can do," Caía said, smiling.

Five

Against eternal injustice,
man must assert justice.
– Albert Camus

CHICAGO, WEDNESDAY, JUNE 15, 2016
NICK

GROGGY AND HUNG OVER, NICK MADE HIS WAY INTO THE OFFICE. At a quarter to eight, the lights were already on and, somewhere, computer keys were clack clacking away, but, yet again, Amy wasn't at her desk. It wasn't like her to be late two days in a row, and he thought perhaps she was feeling the tension. First thing this morning, he meant to talk to her. Good thing Sam was already working on a transfer.

Inside his office, he set his briefcase down without turning on his lights and moved to his desk, wiggling the mouse on his pad to wake the screen. It was precisely where he'd left it last night, on the TravelBot site. Fare to Spain would be around eleven-hundred bucks. Cheap if he booked a month out. More if he took off this weekend . . .

He sat, stretching his legs, slumping into the chair as he stared at the screen.

Laser-thin slivers of light seeped through the closed blinds, casting louvered patterns on the industrial gray carpet.

The flight he'd chosen probably wasn't viable anymore. Having awakened the computer from sleep mode, he was sure that a refresh would return him to the site's search engine, but he didn't touch it yet, not yet . . . because then he would feel compelled to do another search, and what was the point until he knew what to do?

Avoidance wasn't anybody's friend, but it was his brother who tackled life head-on. Nick didn't have his fortitude, nor his natural inclination to take on the world. Deep down, his gut burned with self-reproach. One thing was sure, he was too distracted to work.

Maybe Sam was right to worry.

Marta's face flashed through his head—warm, chocolate eyes, so full of love and acceptance. She was exactly the sort of woman Nick always fancied for himself. He and Jimmy had met her on the same day, on a park bench near the plaza de españa, where she'd been studying for exams. Her personality was so warm and fiery, and that accent . . . Nick adored it from the start. She had this wonderfully archaic way of speaking, especially when she switched to English. Formal, but friendly, and despite this, she cursed like a sailor. If Nick had been the one to catch her flyaway scarf, maybe it would have been him who ended up with her.

Who was he kidding? He had to go. And still, he stared at the screen a good thirty minutes longer, just to be sure. He glanced at the clock, and finding the hour at three past eight, he got up from his expensive desk and made his way down the long hall, toward Sam's office. "Hey," he said, rapping on Sam's door. "You busy?"

Momentarily startled, Sam immediately turned over a document. "Nah," he said, recovering himself. "Come on in."

Ambivalent still, Nick stood in the doorway a moment, and then dove into Sam's office and closed the door. His boss and "future partner" studied him as he sank into the chair facing his desk.

Shaped like a question mark in the middle of the room, with exotic wood inlays and burls, the desk was easily worth twice Nick's desk. In fact, the one they'd recently moved into Paul Savant's office was equally elaborate. Nick brought in more than his share of clients, and more importantly, he kept them happy, but Paul was working on a particularly lucrative account. Nick wouldn't put it past him to have hinted at taking them somewhere else unless he was given the partnership. Sam was greedy enough to buckle. Evidently, their bond of friendship had a double edge. Apparently, Sam took for granted that Nick would stick around.

Alexander Dumas once said, "In business, sir, one has no friends, only correspondents." Nick sensed the truth of those words as he glanced at the document Sam had turned upside down.

Sam pushed the document beneath his computer screen. "Must be serious by the look on your face—hey, if it's about Amy, don't sweat it. Turns out, Paul will be happy to have her. His girl is going on maternity leave soon."

Nick made a pyramid with his index fingers, clasping his hands together, and arching a brow at the mention of his rival for partnership in the firm.

Sam began to massage his jaw. He was ruffled by Nick's presence this morning. In fact, Paul was exactly the sort of guy to move ahead in this business. Not that their transactions were criminal, but it took a special kind of aptitude to look a sixty-year-old widow in the face and take her husband's life insurance money to sink into risky investments. "He's exemplary," Nick agreed, and the irony in his tone wasn't lost on Sam. Once again, Nick glanced at the document Sam had turned upside down, and Sam intercepted his gaze.

"Hey, Nick . . . you know, there's a reason he hasn't been given a partnership yet, same as you . . ."

Nick shook his head, realizing his decision was already made. "This isn't about Paul, Sam. It's not about Amy either."

Sam reached out, nervously clicking the button on his mouse, depressing it two or three times. And then finally, he grabbed the document from his desktop and placed it into a desk drawer, out of sight. "Okay," he said. "Talk."

"I'm going to Spain."

Clearly, that wasn't what Sam expected to hear. His brows collided. "How long?"

"I don't know."

"Jimmy?"

Nick nodded, and so did he.

"All righty, then. So, when will you be back?"

"I don't know."

"Nick . . ." Sam eyed him meaningfully. "You know I can't guarantee anything if you're gone for long? The partners are antsy."

"I get it," Nick said. "Don't worry about it."

"Well, what about the quarterly review for the Busch account?"

Nick's largest and most persnickety account. Despite the fact that they liked Nick, they threatened to leave at least twice a year, and it was only because of Nick that they remained. His challenge was not lost to Sam. "Give it to Paul."

Sam might have been stymied over the partner decision, but anger flashed across his face. He preferred to be the one in charge. "All righty," he said. "Something more I can do?"

Nick stood up. "Nope," he said. "This is something I have to work out on my own."

"All righty, then."

This time, those two curt words were a dismissal. Nick turned to leave but pivoted around once more. "Hey, don't fill Amy's position," he said, in case Sam mistook his meaning.

And that, more than anything, drove home his point. Sam nodded once again, imitating a dashboard Chihuahua. And then he shook his head, as though Nick were making a grave mistake. "Are you sure, Nick?"

"I'm sure."

"All righty. If you're sure."

"I'm sure," Nick said again, and exited the office before he could waffle and change his mind. He walked out, feeling lighter than he had in years. *Fuck the house in Roscoe Village. Fuck the BMW. Fuck the partnership.*

He went back to his office and woke up his computer. For less than a minute, he sat staring at the screen, mulling over his decision one last time, just to be sure. When he couldn't figure a reason not to do it, he performed another search for flights—the same search he'd performed the night before. He found the flight he wanted and bought a ticket—as decisive a move as he'd made in months. There was no more ambivalence now. He was focused and driven.

He didn't bother to clear out his desk. Sam would have it done. Eventually, they would send a courier over with his belongings if that's where it had to go. But he already knew it would.

He grabbed his too-tight jacket from the back of his chair and was out the door, even before lunch. Rather than diddle around, or grab a bite in the building, he made a beeline for his car, intending to go straight home and pack. Food could wait. For the first time in so long, he felt the courage of his convictions—or rather Jimmy's convictions. Because he was the one who'd raised Nick up. It was Jimmy who'd paid for Nick's education. Jimmy who'd stood beside him when their mom died and their dad fucked off. Now it was Nick's job to stand beside his dying brother.

Out in the parking garage, he unlocked his car door, feeling antsy. He fished his cell phone out of his pocket, thinking about what to tell Marta . . . But, no, that conversation could wait. The minute he told her, she would tell Jimmy, and Jimmy was bound to be angry that Nick was putting his life on hold. No, he preferred to have that particular conversation in person.

For six whole months, his brother had kept the knowledge of his illness secret, forbidding Marta to tell him. But his prognosis was certain now, and there wasn't time to mess around.

He tossed his cell phone onto the passenger seat, slightly annoyed that he hadn't bothered to sync it to the onboarding system. He tossed the jacket into the back seat, unconcerned about wrinkling the fabric. "Hang on, bro, here I come," he said, and then slid behind the wheel of his car.

In a rush to be home now, he pulled out of the garage, pressing the gas, not too much, acutely aware of the excitement building deep in his gut. It wasn't joy precisely, because he knew this wasn't going to be easy. It wasn't every day you had to watch a brother die of cancer. But he felt good about his decision, because for once, he was doing something for somebody else.

He was halfway down the street when the cell phone on the passenger seat rang. He glanced over, only for a second. The ring was Jimmy's, but now wasn't the time to talk. He turned around, just a split second later—no more than that. The light was still green. A blur of movement slid in front of his car—a boy on a skateboard.

Nick slammed the brakes. The car's nose dove. His cell phone flew off the seat, popping against the dash. It happened in seconds, only in slow motion. The boy's look of terror. The wide, pale blue eyes and twisting mouth. There was a sickening thud, the sound of flesh and bones breaking as the boy's body flew up and over Nick's hood. The kid's forehead cracked against his windshield, leaving a mess of red and white. It happened so fast. One second, Nick had lifted himself to greatness. The next, with his foot jammed up against the brake and his fingers white and gripping the steering wheel, he was down again. Only this time he'd brought someone else down with him—a boy. And he knew before he put his car into park that the kid was already gone . . .

Six

If you're going through hell,
keep going.
– *Winston Churchill*

JERÉZ, PRESENT DAY

FOR THE SECOND TIME IN LESS THAN A MINUTE, CAÍA SLID HER PHONE OUT OF HER JACKET POCKET, BLINKING AT THE SCREEN. She placed a hand on the massive door, trying to find the nerve to knock. It was six minutes past eight. She didn't have to do this. She could walk away.
You like her, right? Then go away.
What could she hope to gain by going in and disrupting Marta's life? Every time she asked herself this question, the answer grew murkier and murkier.

It had been too long since anyone had reached out to her so genuinely. There was something about Marta that made Caía feel she could understand . . .

Only, not really. No one could truly understand—not unless they too had lost someone near and dear, but some people had a greater affinity to read others, and a knack for making them feel whole again. That was the hope that kept Caía's feet planted to the stoop.

Desperately, she wanted to feel whole again . . . or maybe some semblance of whole. She wanted to taste food again, enjoy a glass of wine. She wanted to envision a future that wasn't . . . this.

Sliding an open palm across the old door, she touched the rough, weathered surface. It was an ancient door. *How long had it been here?* she wondered. How many wistful and grudging pairs of eyes had fallen upon its iron knockers? How many servants had come and gone?

The door was a relic from the distant past. Caía stood in front of it, as intimidated as any who had stood here before her. She balled her hand into a fist and laid her knuckles gently against the wizened wood.

Very likely, the year this house was built, Spain had been in the midst of war. It was an easy assumption. The country had suffered war for most of the eighteenth century—the Carlist wars, wars with Cuba, the Spanish-American War—all those wars that were glossed over during Caía's American history lessons. Marta's great, great grandfather had been an ambassador, she'd said. Which generalissimos had come knocking here? Franco? Probably, his Guardia Civil.

And that tree? Caía peered back at the maple looming behind her, with the sidewalk buckling around its base, its limbs reaching high above the third-floor rooftop. How many servants had taken respite beneath those outstretched limbs, before going to the market? Or waiting for a bus?

The timelessness of inanimate objects and places made Caía's heart ache. Truly ache. Deep, deep down. Her son had been alive no more than an instant in the grand scheme of things, a fleeting breath, and now he was gone. Like the flame of a candle, his life was snuffed out . . . by the man inside this house. Resolved at last, Caía knocked.

When no one came for five minutes or more, she knocked again, this time more firmly. And this time, the door opened. It was Marta who'd answered. "¡Bienvenida! Come in!"

Behind her, a little girl disguised as a pink confection threw up a hand in greeting, showing five fingers. "Tengo cinco," she said. Like her mom's, her eyes were so deep and dark, they appeared to be lined, and her lashes were long and feathery. Her smile was beautiful.

"You're five? What a big girl," Caía said.

The little girl peered up at her mom with a furrowed brow. "Que dice que eres una niña muy grande. Venga, dile tu nombre."

The little girl turned again to Caía, placing a hand behind her back. "Mi nombre es Laura," she said, taking her cues from her mother.

"No, Laura, en inglés."

"My name es Laura," the child said one more time, this time in English. "Today es mi cumpleaños, and I am . . ." She struggled with her fingers, putting all but one up, and then all five. "Cinco."

Caía laughed. There was no need to pretend good humor. Marta's daughter was delightful, with an infectious smile. She had one missing tooth, and Caía couldn't help but remember a little boy with blond hair and bright blue eyes who'd tied a loose tooth to his bedroom doorknob because his father told him to.

"Tonight," Marta said to her daughter, "you will speak only English, Laura. ¿Vale?"

Laura peered up at her mother, brows colliding. "¿Por qué? ¿Porque ella no entiende español?"

"Claro, pero—"

"I do understand Spanish," Caía explained, brandishing a small gift from behind her back. "But I will make you a deal, Laura. You will learn English while I learn Spanish, *vale*? I will be your teacher and you will be mine."

The little girl's eyes brightened at the sight of the unexpected gift, immediately unconcerned with her lessons. "¿Para mí?" She peered up at her mother with a wide-open mouth.

"Yes, for you," Caía said, bending to talk to her. "Thank you for letting me celebrate your birthday, Laura."

The child's shoulders rose with glee as she embraced the small package.

"¿Ahora qué dices?"

"Thank you too much!"

Caía laughed. "You are so welcome."

"Come in," Marta insisted, opening the door a little wider. And to her daughter, she said, "Go and put your regalo en la cocina, Laura. Ábrelo después. Go get your tío Nick. Tell him our lovely guest has arrived."

Caía blinked, not over the compliment.

Uncle Nick?

She blinked again, taken aback by the revelation. It hadn't even occurred to her that Nicholas Kelly might be the child's uncle. That army of fire ants came crawling back, stinging away at the pit of Caía's stomach. Somehow, it didn't seem possible he was here legitimately. Although he could still be mooching off Marta? Simply because he was the child's uncle didn't mean he had come for altruistic reasons. Half dazed, a little off kilter, Caía followed Marta into the house. Once beyond the foyer, it became clear how affluent the family was.

The quiet opulence of the home took Caía's breath away. Much of the first floor was an elaborately tiled courtyard with an indoor pool, complete with a waterfall. Twin lions spouted streams into mosaic bowls. Three stories high, an enormous skylight took center stage on the third-floor ceiling, installed over the fountain-fed pool. The entire edifice reminded Caía of a sultan's bath.

Along the periphery of the courtyard, a number of rooms with massive doors spilled into the massive hall. No fewer than three sitting areas flanked the crystalline pool. In the background, the Spanish guitar of Joaquín Rodrigo strummed softly throughout the house. The back door had been left ajar and, as Caía suspected, it led to a moonlit garden, where the soft glow of a fireplace burned outside, casting its amber light onto the surrounding Spanish tilework.

With Caía's gift in her hands, Laura hurried toward a set of white marble stairs. "¡Tiíto!" she ran shouting. "¡Tiíto!"

"No corras, Laura. ¡Por favor!" her mother said. "Your uncle will be precisely where you left him." She turned back to Caía and said, "She is so . . . emocionada, how you say—excited."

"She is lovely," Caía reassured.

"Thank you, Caía. You have brightened my daughter's day. She has been so sad since her father passed away."

And this, Caía realized suddenly, was the reason for their communion in the market. Both she and Marta had suffered losses, and Marta had effectively said so, except that Caía hadn't been listening. *It is a terrible thing to lose a husband, and more terrible yet to lose a child.*

"Oh, Marta. I am so sorry, I didn't realize," Caía said, chastened by the confession. Her grief embarrassed her, because she had clearly only been thinking of herself.

Marta nevertheless smiled. "My husband has been gone now for nearly one year," she said, holding up a finger, and despite the strong façade, Caía noted a slight trembling of her lips. "Laura's uncle has been a gift to us. I do not know how we will survive without him."

A bit melodramatic, but the revelation had a sobering effect upon Caía. Some part of her wanted to apologize immediately, walk out the front door, and leave these people to live their lives in peace. But she stood a minute too long and "Tiíto" came bounding down the stairs, holding his very excited niece by the hand. Laughing, Laura skipped ahead of him, and only managed not to drag him down for his firm, steady hand and the sheer length of his arm.

Nothing could have prepared Caía for the sight of Nick Kelly up close.

Oh, sure, he was the same guy she'd spied from a distance—with that reddish-blond hair and those fathomless green eyes. But it was his presence she was unprepared for. Once off the steps, Nick Kelly stood a full head taller than Caía, with shoulders that said he worked out. But, yes, of course, he would be so vain, she thought bitterly. He had been a man at leisure for quite some time now. What else would he have to do while waiting for Laura to get out of school? She compared him with Gregg, and tried not to sneer.

It was difficult to view Nick in a positive light, and more difficult yet to meet his gaze, but Caía did so. He extended a hand in greeting, smiling companionably, and Caía was forced to reach out and embrace his gesture. It galled her, though she took his hand in hers, squeezing firmly, imagining it was her fingers wrapped around his throat instead. Only once she locked eyes with him, for one disconcerting moment, she couldn't pry her gaze away.

Both Marta and Laura seemed to disappear from the room, despite the fact that they remained at her side. "I understand you are from Chicago," Nick said, shaking her hand with equal vigor. "Whereabouts?"

"The burbs," Caía said.

His gaze remained steady as he persisted. "Where?"

"Oh, um, Arlington Heights."

"Nice area. So, what brings you to Spain, Caía?"

You, Caía replied silently, in her head. *You did, Nick Kelly.*

"No particular reason. It seemed as good a place as any," she said, and it wasn't entirely a lie. She was managing to do exactly that, despite everything. "Divorce," she added in an effort to quash the conversation.

Neither Marta nor Laura spoke a word. But one glance at Laura's mother revealed an odd glimmer in her eyes. So, this had been her intent all along? To bring two lonely Americans together for supper. Well, the joke was on them.

Guess who's come to dinner, Nico.
Here's a hint, it's not Sidney Poitier.

Caía liked Marta. But this was the most difficult thing she'd ever had to do—stand face-to-face with the man who'd killed her son and not scratch out his eyes. It was for Marta's sake she held herself together. And for Laura's as well. Only belatedly did she realize that she and Nick were still holding hands. She ripped her hand away, rubbing it as though she'd been stung.

"I am so happy," Marta said. "I knew you would get along!" Pleased with herself, she clapped her hands. "Now, we will leave you to become acquainted while we go and check the paella, ¿no? Come along, Laura," she said, before either Nick or Caía could protest her departure.

"Mami, ¿puedo abrir mi regalo?"

"First, let us see if the paella is ready."

"Can we show Eugenia?"

"Despues," Marta said. "We will wait to open your present later, *vale*?"

"*Vale.*"

Hand in hand, mother and daughter disappeared up the same stairs Nick had descended, where Caía assumed the kitchen must be. Uncomfortable to her bones, Caía peered around at the peculiarities of the ground floor. Bars near the front door, more bars near the back door. She felt as though she'd been imprisoned with her enemy, forced to face him. And in a sense, it was true. "Lovely house," she said.

"Yes, it is," Nick agreed. He slid a hand into his pocket as he studied her. "Marta and Jimmy restored it from ruins."

"Oh," Caía said, drifting away from Nick, seemingly nonchalantly, though really she meant to put some much-needed space between them. She could smell him—not a terrible scent, but she didn't want that odor stored in her memory. It was not the cloying scent of expensive cologne, just clean male skin and a slightly toasty scent, as though he'd been warming himself by a fire. This was not what Caía had expected. She didn't know how to stand, what to say, how to be.

"Would you like a tour?"

"No, thank you," Caía said, desperately eying the front door.

"Are you sure?"

Caía shrugged, this time perhaps more uncertainly, and her gaze climbed to the skylight in the ceiling.

"It opens up. Beautiful on a warm summer night. You can stargaze while floating in the pool."

"It's November," Caía said, shivering, grateful no one had offered to take her jacket. She rubbed her arms, despite the temperature being closer to seventy than sixty. More than anything, she wanted to leave now. She didn't want to think of Nick Kelly floating half naked in a Sultan's pool. Somewhere, she thought she heard a clock ticking away seconds, but it was probably in her head. She heard screams, sirens, and for an instant, reality felt disjointed.

There was no way she should be standing here now, arms crossed, counting away the seconds until she could make a dash for the door—particularly not after scheming for months about how to get face-to-face with this man.

"I take it Marta didn't warn you she was playing matchmaker?"

Caía lifted her face to Nick's gaze. "Is that what she's doing?"

He smiled, a smile that might have been charming . . . if Caía didn't already loathe him. "That's my guess. Americans in Spain, both from Chicago. I'm sure she thought we might have some things in common."

Oh, boy, do we ever.

Caía wanted to tell him exactly what it was.

Jack Lawrence Paine, my son.

"She probably feels I've been alone too long."

Yeah, well, so what? So had Caía, and the one thing she'd counted on—because, yes, Marta was right, no parent should ever outlive her child—was that Jack would be around long after Caía was gone. But he wasn't, and she didn't believe anyone could comprehend the concept of loneliness until they faced the loss of a child. A baby that came from her womb. A child she'd raised from his first breath. She'd taught Jack how to walk, talk, and how to brush his teeth. Husbands, boyfriends came and went. *Screw men. Screw relationships. Screw Gregg. Screw this man standing in front of her, with his dental job that must have cost a mint.* Gone might be his suits, but there was no sense of hardship coming from Nicholas Kelly. His black skinny pants were something out of *GQ* magazine, and his blinding white T-shirt made her think of Brad Pitt. Softly woven and tight, it wasn't exactly a working-man's brand. "So, what about you," she asked. "What brings you to Jeréz?"

Moving in on his brother's rich wife, no doubt.

"My brother," he said, exhaling a massive sigh. "Unfortunately, I got here just in time to bury him. Brain cancer."

"Oh," she said in a tiny voice. "How sad." But even hearing that, Caía couldn't give him any credit. She couldn't imagine he'd come here for humanitarian reasons. "How long did you know he was ill?" He must have known about his brother's illness for a long time, and simply missed the opportunity to be at his side because he, like Gregg, was too busy to stop and put time and energy into anyone else.

"About a year, give or take," he said. "But . . ." He fidgeted nervously, lifting a hand to his temple. "Something happened that kept me from coming sooner." There was a shift in his demeanor. A look of raw pain crossed his eyes that he didn't attempt to conceal. It really surprised her. "He was barely cognizant . . . when I arrived. And then . . . once he was gone . . ." He pulled his hand out of his pocket and crossed his arms, precisely the way Caía was doing. Their combined body languages couldn't have been more guarded or unfriendly. "Well, you know, I stayed to help out with my niece—and Marta. I promised Jimmy I would look after them."

Caía didn't want to feel sorry for Nick Kelly. "That makes sense," she said, reading between the lines. She assumed, probably correctly, that the something that happened was Jack's accident. However swiftly they might have conducted Nick Kelly's investigation, she was sure it must have taken some time. There had been no formal charges, or any true investigation, but she imagined they would have asked him to stick around, regardless. Or maybe he had ordained it himself.

Upstairs, she could hear the happy shouts of a little girl, and her mom's ensuing laughter.

"Here," he said. "Let me take your jacket." His tone brooked no argument, and Caía found herself shrugging out of her good leather coat—the only nice present Gregg had ever given her. She handed it over, despite not wanting to. Nick walked away with it and hung it on a coat rack, then returned. "How about that tour?"

"Sure," she said, and gritted her teeth as he placed a hand on the small of her back.

Seven

We must embrace pain and
burn it as fuel for our journey.
— *Kenji Miyazawa*

ONE QUICK TOUR AROUND Nº 5 CALLE LEALAS SERVED TO ILLUSTRATE THAT, NO, INDEED, LIFE COULDN'T BE MORE UNFAIR. How was it that some people lived on the streets and others, like Marta Herrera Nuñez, lived like this? Why was she so special? Why was Nick?

Of course, Caía didn't begrudge Marta her riches. It wasn't that. It wasn't about what either of them had, or didn't have, but their general ability to have it, particularly since some people under this roof were directly responsible for the lack of ability other people had to strive for such things.

So, no, it wasn't that Jack would never have a house like this—he probably wouldn't have chosen it anyhow—it was that he would never be afforded a chance to try, or even to decide whether, for example, a Nasrid dynasty tapestry was an important addition for an already gaudy hall.

Or whether a garishly expensive Persian carpet—probably authentic—was a proper thing to walk on with dirty shoes.

As she passed by, Caía touched a calligraphic plaster fragment on display, wondering if it was an imitation. Spanish Islamic art was lovely, but if Marta possessed such things, they were probably not recent acquisitions. They would be heirlooms, passed down through the ages. The house was a veritable palace, with the second floor being a proper living space, equally as luxuriously furnished as the first floor. But somehow, it managed to feel a bit more lived in, despite the fact that they employed a full-time servant who kept the house spotless. Caía thought perhaps this was because here, on this piso, they were somewhat less formal than their home appeared to be.

Laura came shrieking past, skidding over the hardwood floors with hard leather shoes. She raced back out, carrying a well-dressed blond baby doll by the hair, cackling loudly. She waved the doll and then ducked back into the room from whence she'd come.

It was impossible to say exactly how many rooms the second floor held, but along Caía's tour, she counted ten doors, not including the three balcony doors that opened to the view of the downstairs courtyard. Nick Kelly unlatched one of the balcony doors, opening it up to allow Caía to peer down at the pool. Naturally curious, she slid past him, taking care not to brush against him as she peeked over the balcony. As he'd said, it was a spectacular view.

Caía had never known anyone who lived this way. Her parents had been poor, their accounts of Poland so rife with hardship that they had never once considered taking her "home" for a visit. There were few family photos, but from those that existed, Caía had a sense of scarcity—except for that one photo of Caía's grandmother with the lush fur shawl, taken, perhaps, before Nazi occupation. All Caía knew for certain was that the shawl did not arrive with her mother, and neither did either set of grandparents. Little to nothing was said about their lives, or their deaths, and Caía had learned to respect her parents' silence. Some things were simply not meant to be shared . . .

Like your reason for being here.

"Jim designed the pool for the view," Nick said. He closed the door again, shutting off the sound of trickling of water. One floor closer to the skylight, these doors would invite daylight into an otherwise dark interior.

"So, your brother was an architect?"

"Yes," he said, scratching the top of his ear. But that was all he said before continuing along the tour. As it was below, the second-floor corridor persisted from one end of the house to the other. Street-side, there was an enormous living room, complete with a fireplace that looked like something out of a Jane Austen novel. In that room alone, Caía counted no fewer than three sofas and ten chairs, all grouped together into two seating arrangements. French doors leading to a balcony—presumably the same balcony he'd stood upon earlier today—lay squarely in the middle of the room, closed off at this hour to keep the nighttime street noise from the parlor.

Although no one was seated in this room right now, the fireplace was ablaze, and Caía wondered if this was where Nick had picked up his toasty scent. A glance at the coffee table revealed a sweating mug, half filled with beer. He led her back out of the room, leaving the beer for someone else to clean up, and Caía bristled over that.

At the other end of the hall, the kitchen was large and spacious, with not one but two enormous tables, neither apparently having been intended for the precise use of eating. The centerpiece was a knotty farm table that appeared to be used as a cooking space, judging by the plethora of nicks and scrapes across its surface.

The second table was built in, with a long bench on one side and no seating on the other side. It appeared to be meant for clerical purposes, if the semi-permanent-looking household ledger was any indication—semi-permanent, only judging by its size. Caía could well imagine it must be filled with years and years of annotations. The heavy book had been pushed to one side to make room for Laura's gifts. This is where Caía's last-minute present had found itself, waiting for its time to be unveiled. It sat modestly atop significantly larger packages, all wrapped in pink with silver bows. It wasn't difficult to guess that Laura's favorite color must be pink.

Among these gifts, the flamenco fan Caía had purchased this morning masqueraded as a thoughtful gift, but perhaps not all that appropriate for a five-year-old. The point, however, had been not to arrive empty-handed, but now that she eyed the little package beside the others, Caía wished she'd gone back for one of the artisan dolls.

In the corner, behind the table, hid another set of stairs, leading up to a third floor. Caía assumed this must be intended for the servants. The stairs were dark and uninviting, curling upward and disappearing out of sight. If you closed off the kitchen doors—there were two sets of doors for this purpose—the kitchen area was a self-contained workspace, accessible only from the servant's quarters. The largest set of doors—those leading to the main house—bore speak-easy windows that could be opened from the inside. Yet another door led to the dining room.

Eugenia, a quiet, older woman, with a face generously painted with age spots and bright, unnaturally tinted red hair, moved back and forth between the kitchen and the dining room. This was the same woman Caía had seen on the stoop the other day, locking the front door—a servant after all. And yet Caía was surprised to discover it wasn't Eugenia who was toiling over the stove.

Marta was doing the cooking, with a bit of help from her birthday girl. As Caía and Nick entered the kitchen, Marta peeled off her apron, immediately assuming the role of house mistress. Laura, on the other hand, wearing her own apron, one twice her size, leaned over the table to pluck a slice of chorizo from the cutting board while her mother wasn't looking. The discreet act of defiance reminded Caía of her son . . . and maybe a little of herself. All three of them were only children, and perhaps this was a trait only children shared—a mild but harmless resistance to authority. She and Laura shared a conspiratorial look. The child beamed, a smile that was neither self-assured nor contrite.

"Alas, it will not be my best paella," her mother said apologetically. Without turning to look at her daughter, she said, "Fingers out, Laura. Remember yourself before our guest."

"I didn't do anything, Mami," Laura said, her elbows still on the table as she slid Caía another conspiratorial glance.

Out of practice though she was, Caía gave the child her best "mommy nod" in support of her mother. Seemingly oblivious to their interaction, Marta floated past, opening the dining room door to reveal a space that seemed more appropriate for heads of state than it did for a family of three celebrating a five-year-old's cumpleaños.

"Sit where you wish," Marta said.

"I will have Papá's chair!" Like a Tasmanian devil, Laura raced into the dining room, her pink chiffon dress tickling Caía as she passed. She chose a chair at the far end of the twelve-seater table, while her uncle chose a seat in the middle, and Marta picked the opposite end of the table from her daughter. For her part, Caía felt obliged to choose the seat across from Nick. It was maybe appropriate they should face off. Regrettably, only one of them had any inkling of the undertones present during this standoff.

I want answers, she told him silently.
Do you think of my boy?
Every day? Like I do?
Or have you already forgotten?

After Jack's death, something had broken inside Caía. Gregg's rejection only exacerbated what she was already feeling. She had reassured herself, time and again, that finding Nick Kelly gave her purpose. She had been so sure that someone like him would have subverted justice. A favor here. A favor there. And somehow, men of his ilk never paid for anything at all.

Only now, as Caía sat across from him, instead of the cocksure opportunist she had once expected to encounter, she found a quiet, contemplative uncle whose attention was centered upon his niece . . . occasionally drifting to Caía or to Marta. For the most part, Caía detected a mild curiosity in respect to herself. As for the way he regarded Marta . . . Caía watched them closely, picking up no signs of flirtation. Whatever was between them was . . . uncomplicated.

Eugenia served Marta's paella, dishing out plates from the buffet behind her mistress. On smaller plates, she placed three large shrimp, along with a slice of bread with plenty of spiced oil— gambas al ajillo, Marta explained. Shrimp cooked with garlic. There was more in the kitchen. If Caía wanted more, Eugenia would bring it.

Much to Caía's surprise, she found herself eating, and tasting her food. Contrary to Marta's fears, the paella was delectable. She had criticized her dish nearly the entire meal, and only belatedly did Caía realize she might be fishing for a compliment. "This is fabulous!" she offered.

"Oh, good!" Marta said. "I was afraid I had ruined the socarrat."

By nature, Marta Herrera Nuñez would do nothing less than stellar. Caía sensed this, but she was also not annoyingly overconfident. She was lovely, with her dark olive skin, chocolate eyes, and rich auburn hair—exactly the sort of Spanish woman "cantantes" would croon about. And yet you would never know this by her demeanor—nor by Nick's. If Nick Kelly thought Marta beautiful, he gave no indication he was pining over his brother's widow.

"Really," Caía said. "It's perfect."

"She's a fabulous cook," Nick said, after a long interval of silence. The sound of his voice had the same effect as glass across a tin. It gave Caía a shiver. And yet, as acutely aware as she was of the man seated before her, she studiously avoided his gaze, discomforted by her growing ambivalence toward him. There was a lot she wanted to say, but suddenly face-to-face with him, Caía ate her words as vigorously as she did Marta's paella, confused by the disjointed thoughts that were filtering through her head. She eyed Nick across the table as she bit the tail off a shrimp. Was it crazy to follow a man halfway across a planet to demand answers—to discover for herself whether he'd taken her son's death in stride?

Yes.

Normal people didn't stalk other people. Normal people didn't put their lives on hold and go skim off savings to find out . . . what?

That Nick Kelly was a family man, after all? That, by all accounts, he seemed to be a sweet uncle and a godsend to his dead brother's wife?

Faced with the reality of this family, Caía's intentions were all askew.

But . . . she needed answers . . . if for no other reason, to be sure Jack's death had been more than an inconvenience for him, like a parking ticket left unpaid. She needed to be sure there had been consequences . . . as there had been for her. It wouldn't be fair for him to take her son's life—her life—and go on with his own as though nothing had ever happened.

Because something did happen.

After the dinner plates were all cleared, new dessert plates were set before them, and the cake—a magnificent pink mountain of sugar—was placed in front of Laura.

Once again, Caía wished she'd bought a doll—or something else. The fan she'd brought was a mournful black—hardly a bright and happy color. At least the roses were pink. But it was too late now—just as it was too late to back out of this dinner invitation. Laura clapped her hands together with ill-suppressed glee. "Now, we can finish eating mi pastel, and then, and then, I can open you present," Laura said to Caía.

"Your," Nick corrected. "It signifies possession."

"Ya lo sé," Laura said, tipping her chin up. "I forgotted."

Both mom and uncle peered at one another, smiling between themselves, reluctant to correct the child yet again. They let it go, and it was a good thing—even Jack, whose first and only language had been English, had often confused the idiosyncrasies of words.

Me don't want that, he would say. *Me don't want it, Mommy.* For the longest time, it had been impossible to get him to understand the difference between *me* and *I*, and this had persisted until he was four. "I don't want it, Jack," Gregg would correct him, his tone harsh.

"Gregg."

"Don't Gregg me, Caía. The boy's gotta learn the right way to talk. He can't go 'round yammering like a Muppet."

Wide-eyed, Jack had sat there, looking from Gregg to Caía and back again to Gregg. He was only three at the time, and Caía liked the way her son talked. He would outgrow it soon enough, but for the time being, she only wanted him to feel confident and speak freely. She and Gregg had different ideas about how to inspire a child. Was it any wonder they'd never had another?

In Laura, Caía recognized none of the telltale shyness Jack had displayed at her age. Laura sat straight, hands away from her mouth, eyes wide, ready to participate in the discussion—also surprising for the simple fact that it was after 10:00 p.m. They were only now finishing up dinner. Back home, meals were never served at this hour. Kids were more likely than not brushing their teeth and getting ready for bed. Or, in Jack's case, pretending to be asleep, playing with his cars beneath the covers. Or dismantling a radio or a watch. One time, he'd ruined Caía's headphones, plucking off the rubber ends and sticking toothpicks into the speakers, because he said he wanted to see how big the speakers were.

"Do you know what?" Laura said. "My tiíto gaved me tacones rosas."

"For your birthday?"

Laura nodded enthusiastically, and Caía looked to Marta, who seemed to understand that Caía needed clarification. "Pink flamenco shoes. She has wanted them so long."

The image of Nick Kelly picking out a pair of child's tap shoes did not appeal to Caía. "No pony?" she joked, sliding Nick a challenging glance.

Laura's brow furrowed and her head slid back, as though she thought the suggestion perfectly ridiculous. "We cannot have any ponies," she said, looking at her mother. And then, she asked Caía, her voice rising an octave, "Did you have a pony when you was a baby?"

This time, Caía took care not to look at Nick. "Uh, no."

Laura clapped her hands together. "Ohhh! I know why." She held up a hand, as though to be called on in class, but she didn't wait. She blurted out, "Because you did not afford any ponies! My mami says we don't have any monies."

"Laura! Please—ay, dios mío! You must excuse my daughter," Marta said to Caía, even though the fault was

Caía's more than Laura's for introducing such a snide remark to begin with—a dig at her uncle with unintended results. "She is quite presumptuous. Of course, we get by, though it has been difficult. A house this size is quite demanding."

Like a magnet, Nick Kelly drew Caía's gaze. He had said very little throughout supper, but Caía was aware that he was listening to every word, studying Caía, but to what end, she hadn't any clue, because his thoughts remained his own. The tension was murdering her, so she'd baited him. He never took the bait. He kept right on eating and thinking his private thoughts.

"I'm sure," Caía said, feeling muddled. It wasn't her intent to involve other people in this exercise, but here she was . . . and there they were . . .

"In fact," Marta said, "I have often thought about selling this house, but it would pain me so much to lose a piece of my history and my heart. Siéntate, Laura," she finished, waving her daughter down into her chair. She was growing impatient for her presents.

Caía slid another glance at Nick, certain he must have come to Spain with plenty of his own money. She knew him to be successful at his job. But if he wasn't going to share his money, a house this size, partitioned as it was, would seem the ideal rental opportunity.

There were at least two bedrooms downstairs, and the first floor was used only to greet guests, as far as she could tell. It was a sad waste, really. No wonder Marta had brought up the history of her home this morning. She must be worried about how to keep it, although as hardships went, it really didn't rate on a scale from one to ten. She could house an entire homeless shelter beneath this roof. "Have you considered renting . . . downstairs?" Caía asked. "Everyone is doing it now. There's even a website . . ."

"Yes, yes, I know. Alas, I have been reluctant to open our home to strangers . . ." And then suddenly Marta squinted her eyes, and said, regarding Caía with a wily smile, "However, if I knew someone, maybe then I would welcome the company . . ."

It appeared to be a question. Marta inclined her head. "How long did you say you would be in Spain, Caía?"

For the moment, Nicholas Kelly's attention remained on his empty dish.

"I didn't."

"There is a large suite downstairs. It has been vacant now for years."

Silence.

"Oh, yes! Yes! Yes!" Laura said, clapping her hands enthusiastically. "If you live with me, then we can be friends."

And then suddenly everyone was looking at Caía, including a hopeful brown-eyed five-year-old with a dab of frosting on her upper lip. The cake had yet to be served, but that hadn't stopped Laura from sneaking a taste.

"Now that I think of it, if you would like to rent this room, I could provide a discount . . . perhaps as compensation for helping my Laura practice her English?"

"Oh, yes, yes, yes, yes!" Laura said again, dancing in her chair and kicking her feet wildly beneath the table. Already, she was suffering the effects of too much sugar, and she hadn't even been served a slice of her cake. She threw her hands into the air and Caía thought she might have done the "dab," except that Caía wasn't really sure what the "dab" was.

Evidently, the child had too few friends. Caía struggled to remember if Jack had been so inclined toward adults. Aside from Caía, she didn't believe so.

Everyone was looking at Caía, waiting for her response, and Caía found herself unable to speak. The offer . . . well, it was like putting a child in a candy store, along with a plate full of candy, and saying, "Don't eat it." But Caía wasn't a child. She was an adult who understood right from wrong. Moving in with this family without confessing the truth was inherently wrong. Not telling them she had come to Spain looking for Nick Kelly was also wrong. But she couldn't stop herself from asking, "How much?"

Marta blinked, as though Caía's easy capitulation surprised her. "Well, let me see . . . I believe we could spare it for two hundred euros."

Caía's brows lifted at the modest price—much, much less than she was paying at her current location down the street. "Two hundred per week?"

"No, no, per month," Marta clarified. "And, please, you must say yes, if this suits you. Tu compañía me encantaría, and Laura too." She glanced at Nick, and although she didn't include him, Caía realized she meant to include her brother-in-law as well.

I take it Marta didn't warn you she was playing matchmaker?

There was a tiny telltale smirk playing over Nick Kelly's lips. Evidently, he wasn't the least bit aggravated by Marta's offer, nor surprised by it, but neither did he bother to speak up to encourage it. He remained silent, tinkling his fork against the golden rim of his dessert plate.

Caía was paying a thousand euros now, for a small room in someone else's house—a much smaller place than this. After weeks of living there, she had yet to get to know her landlords. If she accepted this generous offer, she would be trading total strangers for Marta and her daughter . . . and Nick Kelly. Once again, Caía glanced over at Nick, catching his eye. The two held gazes for a long moment. Being this close to him might give her an opportunity to work up the nerve to confront him once and for all . . . except that, deep down, a voice cautioned against the decision, warning Caía that no good could come of her deception, especially where only one party understood the full gravity of the occasion. She heard Lucy's voice again. *No good will come of it, Caía.*

"I'll be happy to look at the room again," Caía said.

"Wonderful!" Marta exclaimed, just as Eugenia re-entered the room, carrying a box of matches in her hand. The maid glanced over at Caía as she slid past Nick, moving purposefully toward the cake. She opened the box of matches, took out a match, and struck it against the side of the box, glancing over at Caía before setting the flame to the wick.

Eight

No one ever told me that
grief felt so like fear.
– *C. S. Lewis*

LIFE HAD A TWISTED SENSE OF HUMOR.
For all the card-toting Southerners—especially those whose ancestors once supported the slave trade—the joke was on them. Along with their payload from Africa arrived a stowaway—the cockroach. And for all that slavery had been abolished now for centuries, those nuclear-bomb-surviving creepy-crawlies had been free from day one—free to infest at will.

The year after Caía moved to Chicago, when she was six months pregnant with Jack, they'd gone home to visit Gregg's parents for his birthday. In Athens, his mother kept a substantial garden, and every harvest, without fail, the house would be filled with crates and crates of fresh vegetables—tomatoes for the most part. This was both awesome and horrific at once.

On the one hand, the taste of Mrs. Paine's tomatoes was heavenly—a fact that even a mostly unforeseen and unwanted newcomer to the family couldn't deny. Of course, Caía was Polish, and her parents were Polish. Her grandparents had been Polish. And what was worse, they were Catholic as well. And Catholic, in case you didn't know, was a dirty word in a Baptist household. So, while her own mother also kept a garden, it wasn't nearly so grand as Mrs. Paine's—yes, Mrs., not Miss, Ms., or even Janet. Because Caía was an underling, and calling elders by their first names was not an acceptable option. Also, Mrs. Paine was a married woman and proud of it. She wasn't into all that women's lib nonsense. "I'm not a Ms., I'm a Mrs. And this attitude is precisely what is ruining the nation's morals," she'd proclaimed. "Caía, I do hope you won't join that bandwagon," she'd said that night during supper.

For years Caía wanted desperately to gain "Gram's" approval. That was the name they'd settled on, because there was a grandbaby on the way, and this, after all, was the family Caía had embraced, despite their refusal to embrace hers.

Her parents were never invited for holidays, and certainly never for Gregg's birthday, despite them coming all the way from Chicago and only having a few days to visit. However, that was not the point here. The point was that as much as it annoyed Caía to admit it, those fat, juicy tomatoes had more flavor than her mother's tomatoes, but all that bloaty, moist, dripping mess drew scores of roaches, and those six-legged creatures scurried over vegetables, laying eggs everywhere. And some of those crates happened to be stacked in the dining room—a fact that Gram seemed unfazed by, despite some of those stowaways knowing how to fly. They buzzed overhead, drunk on tomato bloat, and as they dined together on this particular visit, Caía found herself dry heaving over the sight of two roaches in flight—not one, but two.

Accustomed to the spectacle, the family chatted on, never addressing the cockroaches in the room. Not even Gregg seemed to notice—or if he did, he never acknowledged it to Caía. Vomit seemed imminent. For the entire meal Caía had willed herself, "Don't do it, Caía. Don't do it." And through sheer determination she'd managed not to toss up her guts into the chicken casserole, but she'd salivated uncomfortably up until the time his parents walked them to their car to say good-bye. The very instant Caía heard the screen door slam shut, Caía turned and hurled into the next-door neighbor's azaleas. It was as though the sound of the slamming door had been her cue.

Willpower was a superpower, she'd discovered. Willpower could stop hearts from beating, as in the case of heartbroken old folks. Except that, if you thought about old people dying of loneliness, it was usually the man. So long as there was anyone left to care for, women weren't afforded the luxury of hanging up their spurs. However, simply because you didn't die, didn't mean you didn't wish you had. It also didn't prevent you from feeling guilty for remaining among the living. This—her current situation—was essentially a symptom of her despair. Caía realized this, but having clarity didn't make it any easier to change the course she'd charted for herself. This was the long way of saying that there was no way Caía could turn down Marta's offer.

She wanted answers. More than anything, she wanted answers. But Caía needed something else as well . . . something she couldn't put a finger on. She sensed it had nothing to do with revenge. Sure, she'd like to imagine Nick suffering—or dead—but it was nothing more than a sordid fantasy. Having come face-to-face with Nick Kelly—having had his hand upon the small of her back—no matter how confusing her feelings might be, Caía realized there was no way she could be the catalyst to bring him harm. In fact, wheedling its way into her consciousness even now was an annoying worm of guilt, making her feel—brace yourself for it—sorry for him.

But why?

Whatever, it simply wasn't possible to walk away—not when, for the first time in so long, Caía was feeling . . . something. And this was the point she was . . . feeling.

However, she didn't give Marta an immediate answer, despite already knowing what she planned to do. She gave them all, including Nick Kelly—including herself—the pretense of thinking it over. Exercising great willpower, Caía gave herself a week.

But something odd happened the following morning that changed her mind. She found herself back at Rincon, at her usual table, only as it happened, not during her usual hour—the hour during which Nick Kelly might be walking his niece to school.

On this morning, Caía showed up around 10:00 a.m., and when she took her seat, she proceeded to peruse the café menu, wondering what to eat. Yep, that's right; she was starving. Last night's meal had awakened something—what exactly, she didn't know, but there it was.

Unfortunately, the morning choices weren't all that diverse. Jamón ibérico and bread. You could have this one thing with aceite de oliva, or you could have it with mantequilla roja—a spicy Crisco-like spread that came with or without what amounted to be liverwurst. Or, you could have tostada, which had no relationship at all to the Mexican variety. It was simply bread, two pieces, slightly toasted. Caía ordered hers with jamón. Her usual waiter took her order, and he smiled at her unexpected interest in the menu, answering all her questions patiently.

He returned a short time later, with a steaming cup of café con leche, and he brought with him a sample of mantequilla roja for Caía to taste. "Gracias," she said.

"De nada," he returned. "Está muy rico," he assured her. "Eet es very good," he said. And just in case Caía didn't understand, he placed a hand to his lips and kissed the tips of his fingers. "Muy bueno," he said, again.

Caía nodded, picking up the knife as he turned away. She was spreading her mantequilla roja—which wasn't red at all but some peculiar shade of orange—when Nick Kelly spotted her from across the street. Caía noticed him nearly at the same time. She held her breath as he crossed the road. He was coming straight toward her. So, as life would have it, she had come here countless times before, each time looking for him—hoping to work up the nerve to finally confront him—and now, the one time he wasn't on her mind, at least not predominately, he was nevertheless heading her way.

"Good morning," he said. He was dressed in faded blue jeans today, with a powder-blue T-shirt that made him look more tanned than he was. In truth, he was no more so than Caía, after sitting out in the sun—at this very café—every day for the past three weeks.

"Umm . . . good morning," Caía said. Her hand tightened about the knife she held in her hand. She wondered idly how hard she'd have to stab if she meant to do so. She smiled up at him and set the knife down as he stood looking down at her. After an awkward moment, Caía was forced to offer him a seat.

"Don't mind if I do," he said, and promptly sat.

Caía wasn't sharing her food this morning, but the pigeons might have recognized her because they swarmed around her table. The sight of them made her cheeks burn. What if the waiter said something to give her away? What if Nick already knew she was a regular here? What if he'd spotted her on another day during his walk home, despite the fact that his gaze never lingered?

Caía avoided Nick's gaze for a long, uncomfortable moment, tucking away her secrets, and then she finally tilted up her head. "Funny we should meet here."

"Yeah," he said. "Funny."

Why did that seem so full of innuendo?

"Actually, Caía, I was hoping to run into you," he said as the waiter reappeared. Caía held her breath as he ordered a café cortado before returning to his confession . . .

"It's been a while since I've seen Marta so happy," he said. "Whatever you two talked about yesterday—whatever the connection you made, she likes you. A lot."

"Well . . . that's . . . great. I like her, too," Caía said, taking a bite out of her tostada. And it was true. Her dislike of Nick Kelly needn't preclude any positive feelings for Marta. They were not the same person, after all, and Marta had nothing to do with Jack's death. Neither did Laura.

"She's in a vulnerable place," he continued.

Caía nodded, listening. Chewing.

"I sense you two are kindred spirits in more ways than one . . ."

Caía furrowed her brow, swallowing. "Really? What do you mean?"

"Well, I don't know . . . it's just a feeling," he said.

"Well, we definitely connected."

"Yeah, well . . . that's why I hope you'll go ahead and rent that room downstairs."

Caía screwed her face. "You do?"

"Yes."

"Why?"

He winked at her. "Because it's empty," he said, grinning winsomely. The sight of that smile might have even disarmed Caía if only she didn't realize who he was: her son's murderer.

Vehicular homicide. Wasn't that what they'd called it? Regardless of where guilt might lay, that was, in fact, the official name of a traffic investigation.

Unfortunately, to be found guilty of vehicular manslaughter—which was not the same as vehicular homicide—one had to be found criminally negligent, a fact that worked in Nick Kelly's favor. Witnesses to the accident all claimed he wasn't negligent. How fortunate for him.

It changed nothing for Caía.

Caía forced herself to return a smile. Whatever appetite she'd had before Nick's arrival was gone now. Still, she coerced herself into taking another bite, if for no other reason than to have a reason not to have to talk. In the meantime, Nick sat patiently, watching Caía eat, and all Caía could think was, *How rude. How rude!* Any other time, had they been dating perhaps, she might have thought it charming that he wore that tiny smile as he observed her—maybe even somewhat admiringly. But this minute, all she could think was, *How rude.*

"I hope you'll forgive me for being so frank," he said. "I sense you like Marta a bit more than you like me . . . I hope you won't let your dislike for me affect your decision."

"I don't know why you would say such a thing," Caía returned. Like a hypocrite, she shook her head in denial. "I don't know you well enough not to like you." She snapped another bite of her toast, wishing she hadn't stopped chewing long enough to utter big fat lies.

Nick Kelly regarded her more curiously yet as the waiter returned, setting down his steaming cup of espresso. Unlike Caía's, his "leche" was formed into the shape of a heart, and her gaze was drawn inside to the woman standing behind the counter, wondering if the gesture was by accident. Caía didn't get a heart. In fact, she came here every day, and she'd never once gotten a heart.

"Call it a feeling," Nick said.

"Well, don't worry, I've already decided," Caía announced. *Do you know who I am?* she asked silently. *Look into my eyes, Nick Kelly. Do you know who I am?*

"And?"

She held Nick's gaze so long that the steam from his coffee dissipated. She shrugged as though her decision meant nothing. "Why not?"

"As in you'll take it?"

"Well, I don't see why not," she said again.

His answering smile appeared genuine. "That's great," he said, taking a sip from his cup. "Marta won't admit as much, but the truth is that she needs the extra money as well as the friendship. A bit of rent coming in will go a long way."

"The room is worth more than two hundred euros," Caía told him, maybe to ease her conscience over the probability of taking advantage.

"True, but she won't take any more," he said. "Don't worry. She's working again. Two hundred extra euros a month goes a long way here."

Caía held his gaze. "What about you?"

He seemed to realize what Caía was asking. *What about you? Why don't you help provide for them? Isn't this why you're here, after all?* He shrugged. "I do what I can."

Do you, really? Well, he could work in Spain with a proper visa, if he chose to, but she supposed it made more sense for Marta to work in her own country. Certainly, it wasn't Nick's responsibility to raise his niece and fund his dead brother's household. The fact that he was willing to play nanny for Laura should go at least part way toward redeeming him, but Caía preferred to think of him as a mooch. She picked up the top layer of her tostada and glared at the salted ham. "So . . . what does she do?"

"Marta?"

"Yeah."

She could read the pride in his voice as he answered. "She's a marine engineer, teaching at the University of Alicante, León, Cadiz."

Caía's brows lifted. "Wow." She swallowed. "Impressive." So now who was the slacker? Certainly not Marta. It put things into perspective, since Caía was the one who'd once had high hopes, and sold them all away for a nice, soft couch in Roscoe Village. Parenting wasn't easy, but Marta somehow seemed to be mastering that as well—with a dead husband and a precocious child, at that.

"She took time off after Jimmy's death," he was saying. "But now she's back to it."

Caía peered up at Nick through her lashes. She dropped her bread. "So, you stayed to help with Laura?"

He scraped a thumbnail over a spot on his chin, the sound chafing like sandpaper. "Partly."

And what's the other part? Caía wanted to know. She narrowed her eyes. "So . . . you don't believe it's odd renting rooms to strangers when you don't even know their last name?"

He smiled reassuringly. "Did your current landlord do a security check before renting space to you? Should we?" He arched a brow.

Caía blushed, peering into his coffee cup. His foam heart was still intact, despite his initial sip. "No. I rented online. She took my info when I arrived."

"So, we'll do the same. Anyway, we're no longer strangers, are we? You can't exactly call someone a stranger after you've shared a meal."

"I suppose not," Caía said, her eyes still fixed upon his coffee cup. She had the greatest desire to stick her finger in his cup and destroy his pretty little heart.

He thrust his hand out, as though to greet her. "Why don't we get formal introductions out of the way . . . Nick Kelly . . . you?"

Caía swallowed at the sight of the hand intruding upon her space. Not dirty necessarily, but covered with tiny marker stains in various colors—the most predominant being red. *Like blood.* How ironic, because he had blood on his hands already—her son's blood. Hesitantly, she reached out to grasp his hand. "Caía Nowakówna."

His brows drew together. "Is that your married name?"

"No," she said, withdrawing her hand. He didn't get to know any more than that. Despite now having been a good time for disclosures, Caía couldn't bring herself to speak the name she knew would give her away.

Paine. Paine. Paine.
My name is Caía Paine.
Do you know me now?

"Anyway, I'm glad you're taking the room." Pushing his chair back, he then stood.

"Yeah," Caía said. "Me too."

"I'm sorry for intruding." He picked up his cup of coffee and gulped it down. He then set the cup back down on the table, nearly empty, and fished out his wallet, taking out too much money, and tossing the euros down on the table. "It'll be great to have a fellow expat under the same roof," he said, and winked at Caía. "Breakfast is on me, Caía Nowakówna. I'll see you soon."

Nine

It's so much darker when a light goes out than it would have been if it had never shone.
— *John Steinbeck*

JERÉZ, PRESENT DAY

REALLY, DON'T JUDGE.

Given the hand Caía had been dealt, she would have made all the same choices again, albeit maybe not so easily if all her life's possessions hadn't been relegated to a single suitcase. Admittedly, it was maybe too easy making decisions on the fly, and while she would have liked to believe it was a wise decision to pare down her belongings to only those things she knew she couldn't live without, she had been running on compulsion rather than logic, and the contents of her suitcase proved as much. *Like, who needed a Micro Machine car?*

She'd carried the small red pickup in her purse for so long, after discovering it upside down beneath the leg of the living room couch. She'd had the truck in her pocket that morning when she'd learned Jack made it into New Einstein's Academy. It was her good luck charm, she'd decided, and she'd tossed the toy into her purse. Now that Jack was gone, it was more precious than ever.

She'd also brought along a scarf her mother knitted for her when she and Gregg moved to the Windy City, along with a rosary and prayer book Caía hadn't opened since her first communion at the age of twelve. Given the epoch since she'd last opened the prayer book, she couldn't claim to be the least bit religious, but these were things that reminded her of her mother.

For all the rest of her belongings, there was a storage unit in Chicago with Caía's name on it, prepaid for a year, but at this point, she was so far removed from everything in her prior life that she didn't have the least bit of anxiety over the thought of losing it all. Here's the thing: Once you lost the one thing that ever meant anything to you, the value of everything else paled in comparison.

This was also true: While Caía couldn't have cared less if they had taken the lock off her storage unit and offered a free-for-all to the entire city of Chicago, inasmuch as there was no real attachment there, she was inexplicably drawn to all three of N° 5's tenants, for reasons that couldn't possibly be all the same. If Caía had to take a gander, she might try, but if she thought about it too long and hard, she might never follow through.

Therefore, weak willed where this particular effort was concerned, Caía arrived at N° 5 Calle Lealas around 11:00 a.m., and was promptly installed in the biggest of the downstairs suites, an enormous private quarter that included a spacious bathroom, a bedroom, a foyer with closets, and a nook outside the bedroom, on the fringes of the pool. If Caía were inclined to, she might even pretend she was here on vacation, although she wasn't in that frame of mind. It was more like this: She was a spy, a double agent, searching for the truth.

Then again, if she'd had the mind to analyze any of it— especially the double agent analogy—she would have further examined her own growing ambivalence where Nick Kelly was concerned. But she didn't.

The entry to her suite lay hidden behind chunky palms and creeping vines. A bit less camouflaged than the breakfast nook was a small seating area, also near the pool, complete with a wicker sofa, two wicker chairs, and a wicker and glass coffee table. But, really, these were all extensions of her room.

On the coffee table lay magazines, all in Spanish: *Vanidades*, which was probably Marta's; *Siempre Mujer*, also probably Marta's; and *Ser Padres*—a parenting magazine that she couldn't fathom Nick Kelly had ever opened even once. In fact, all these magazines were barely handled, which only made Caía feel none of them had ever been read by the occupants of this house. Their position on the table further encouraged this theory. Positioned so that the spines faced the sofa, they were displayed in a perfect fan shape—like the Spanish fan Caía had given to Laura.

What was more, all the magazines were current. No old periodicals amidst the bunch. And this, Caía decided, must be Eugenia's handiwork—the maid who lived up on the third floor.

For someone who needed the extra money, magazines were a wasted effort, but Caía would certainly make use of them to tighten her Spanish—except for the parenting magazine, which she would never touch. Thanks to Nick Kelly, those articles didn't pertain to Caía anymore.

At any rate, she had rented much worse places for two hundred euros a day, much less two hundred a month, and if she wasn't going to feel guilty about the reason she was here, she certainly didn't intend to feel guilty about the cost of her room. Given that she was working with a fixed income—the proceeds from the sale of her parents' home—the price suited her just fine.

Left to her own devices, it took her all of five minutes to unpack. Her favorite clothes took up less than an eighth of the closet space allotted to her, and her underwear occupied a single drawer. She had three pairs of shoes: a pair of Doc

Martens boots, a pair of sandals, and a pair of pseudo heels. She placed them all on the shelf beneath her clothing, then positioned the prayer book on the bedside table. Marta was very likely Catholic, she thought, and if she saw these things, she would assume Caía was God-fearing as well. More to the point, if she saw these things, she would never suspect Caía of anything—certainly not this.

Stalker, screamed a voice inside her head. She ignored it, hanging her scarf on a wooden hanger. The Micro Machine she left in a drawer, away from prying eyes, along with her iPad. She put both these items inside her dresser, with the iPad turned off. The iPad was her one remaining connection to her prior life, containing access to all her photos of Jack, and all her pertinent information. Although she used to use it to read, she never did that anymore. Her books were forgotten, her music neglected. Her interest in anything that didn't pertain to her son—or Nick Kelly—was nonexistent.

For the first few nights after her arrival, Caía intended to keep to herself, to maybe get her bearings, but Marta seemed intent upon drawing her out, inviting her to dinner, and generally appealing to her better nature for help in the kitchen.

Caía didn't mind; these were moments she felt free to be herself, when Laura and Nick were otherwise occupied, and she and Marta seized the opportunity to commiserate. Only someone who'd lost someone near and dear could understand how Caía felt. At least this is what she told herself when she gave in to the very real yearning for Marta's company.

Even so, there was no pretense in her desire to spend time with Marta. Marta was a kindred soul. Marta understood when she needed to be alone. And if Caía ever chose not to join her, she never had to go up to the second floor, or see another soul. The house was big enough to get lost in. And sometimes, she pretended she was only a renter, and that she and Marta had met only by chance. People did meet that way, she reasoned—perfect strangers who later became dear, dear friends. Marta was precisely that sort of person—the sort of person who was warm and open, hugging everyone, with nothing to hide.

Unlike Caía.

Downstairs, on the patio, there was a fully equipped kitchen. And there was a "tele" room as well, except the TV in that room was ancient CRT technology, by the looks of it from the late eighties or early nineties. The twelve-inch TV was ungainly and wide, taking up most of the space on the cart. Evidently, television was not a priority in this house.

Her son had had a million remotes in his room—under his bed, on top of his dresser, inside his drawers, in the closet—so many Caía had lost track to what device each belonged. That was, after all, why she'd bought him his first skateboard. She'd meant to encourage him to spend more time outdoors. Naturally, he'd gravitated to the skateboard. He and his friends had spent hours digging up her backyard, building ramps. And then Gregg went and bought him that damned cell phone....

Caía pushed the thought away, keeping the darkness at bay.

During the day, there was plenty of light in the main courtyard. But, at night, the skylight did little to illuminate the interior of the house. Tonight, all three upper balcony doors had been left wide open, and though it was getting too cool to swim, it didn't appear to affect the uncle and niece as they horsed around in the pool below. Laughter echoed throughout the house, bouncing off old plaster walls. "No, Tiíto—noo!" Laura squealed.

On the way out of the kitchen, Caía stopped to watch them, hanging back in the shadows so as not to be so obvious.

Alone with his niece, Nick Kelly's serious demeanor softened. He grabbed Laura by one ankle, dragging her into the pool, growling like a monster.

Are you a monster, Nick Kelly?

Living here, maybe she would find out.

Laura shrieked, though not with fear, and Caía found herself thinking back to Jack's childhood. Her husband had been too busy most of the time—even before the affair—and often it was only her and Jack for supper. They too had played together, right up until the time he'd grown bored of playing with Caía. "*Vroom. Vroom. Vroom,*" she would say, rolling cars onto pretend freeways.

"No, Mommmmeee, that's not how they sound," he would correct her with such disapproval. "Cars don't go *vroom, vroom, vroom.*"

"What do they do then?"

"They don't make any sound 'less humans honk."

"Honk, honk," Caía had said with a grin.

"No, no, no!" Once again, he'd pushed her hand away from the car she'd been playing with. "A car only honks when a human is in the way."

"But I am a human," she had complained with a persistent smile.

"Mommeee!"

"Okay, okay, I get it now. Cars only honk for humans?"

"And cows," he'd said with conviction, and Caía laughed.

"It's twu, Mommeee."

"What about chickens?"

Jack shook his head. "No, chickens don' cwoss woads."

"Then how do they get to the other side?"

Her son had looked at her then, completely bemused—perhaps the way Caía was now staring down at the man wading in the pool below.

Did you honk, Nick?
Did you see my son crossing that road?
Why didn't you stop?
Why? Why? Why?

Over and over, in her head, Caía tried to piece together Jack's final moments, and every time she tried to envision it, a sense of panic overwhelmed her, begging her not to see.

Don't look, Caía. Don't look.

Schadenfreude . . . wasn't that what they called it when people drove by, rubbernecking accidents? Try as she did to forget, Caía could hear the doctor's voice in her head, disjointed and hollow, because she had been drinking that day—something she rarely did.

"The spine was compromised at the C-1 and C-2 vertebrae, here and here," he'd said, pointing at a diagram, his words formal and cold. "This is the area that controls the heart and lungs . . ."

"My husband was an architect," Marta said quietly, startling Caía, coming up beside her, and peering down at the "humans" wading in the pool below. "I have always loved this view."

For a moment, they stood together, watching the horseplay, and Marta shook her head. "I don't know what I would do without Nico," she confessed in that thick but proper accent. Her voice was full of raw emotion. "He is the best of the best of the best," she said, using the same phrase she'd used for her olive oil.

Caía slid a glance at Marta's face, catching an honest look of admiration, and felt . . . more discombobulated than ever. *How could that man, down there, be the best of the best?*

Marta turned to look at her, smiling. "You know, I believe he admires you, Caía."

Caía had to catch herself before she could frown. "Me?"

"Well, yes, he said to me that he thinks you are lovely."

Caía pretended an interest in the nonexistent dirt beneath her nails. "Did he?"

"Yes. That first night . . . when you came to my house for dinner. I confess I did ask him when you left. He said he loved your nose."

Caía lifted a brow. "My nose?"

"Yes." Marta smiled companionably. "He said it reminded him of someone he knows."

Caía averted her gaze. Jack had had her same nose, but Caía was certain that couldn't be it. She didn't know how clearly he could have seen her son's face . . . but . . . then . . . maybe . . .

After the accident, they wouldn't allow Caía inside to identify Jack's body—only Gregg. And even after the makeup artist had finished with Jack's body, they'd opted for a closed casket instead. Gregg had insisted Caía not look inside. Only had she been better, she would have fought that edict . . . because now she needed closure.

Blinking down at the pool, Caía remembered her mother's funeral. Initially, her dad had considered cremation, but anxiety over the decision had gotten the best of him and he'd changed his mind at the last minute. Entirely by accident, Caía followed him inside. Her mother lay on that table, the tips of her fingers turning black . . .

She understood exactly what happened to a body after death. She remembered her biology. Sometimes, she wished they had cremated Jack, because now she pictured her son with empty sockets for eyes and skin melting off his bones. It wasn't an image any mother should have to entertain. It was easier to pretend he wasn't gone.

At her side, Marta reached over to squeeze Caía's arm—a gesture that was becoming very familiar. For the first week after moving into the room downstairs, after the dishes were done, she and Marta had retired to the upstairs salon, chatting endlessly, til late at night, about everything from failed marriages to the rearing of children. But they rarely spoke about Jack's death, even though Caía sensed Marta's willingness to listen. Caía couldn't talk about it, not yet—not the details. Probably because she feared she might reveal too much.

"Soon we will make a journey to Zahara," Marta said quietly. "I hope you will join us."

Marta rubbed a hand across Caía's back in that very soothing way mothers had with their young, and Caía found herself leaning into it. "Zahara?"

"Zahara de la Sierra—a little white village in the mountains. And perhaps after we can drive to Baena and you can see for yourself where the best aceite is made."

"You and Laura . . . and Nick?"

"Yes," she said. "It will be one year since we lost my Jaimito. Mi pobrecito."

"I'm sorry," Caía said, but she didn't at once accept the invitation. It was a generous offer, one that illustrated the depth of their unexpected connection—that Marta would wish to share this special anniversary with Caía. But Caía neither deserved it, nor was she comfortable with it.

"Of course, you are welcome to remain in Jeréz, but I hope you will not. It will be nice to share this memorial with someone who understands my pain."

Caía's eyes brimmed with tears as she peered at Marta. Without comprehending her own need for the hug, she reached out and embraced her new friend, and the two stood cradling one another in the upstairs balcony, neither in much of a hurry to let go. Laughter filtered up from the courtyard, the sound entirely discordant with the moment.

Ten

I don't think of all the misery,
but of all the beauty that remains.
— *Anne Frank*

THE KITCHEN SMELLED OF SEAFOOD, SPICES, AND WARM, FRESH BREAD. The frenetic sound of a flamenco guitar filtered in through the open window from the stereo on the terraza below.

Snacking on cheese and jamón and sipping wine as they cooked, Caía and Marta giggled like schoolgirls as the real child stood, perched upon a kitchen chair, supervising the cooking like a duenna. Laura's conspicuousness in the kitchen was not only tolerated but welcome, and every now and again, Marta handed the five-year-old a glass to sip from, pulling it back when Laura drank too deeply. It should be old news by now, but the sight of Laura's hands wrapped about the sides of a wine glass never ceased to surprise Caía. If they should happen to go out for a drink, or take in a flamenco show, Laura always tagged along. Together they'd become a gleesome threesome. It felt so good to laugh. Wiping her eyes and lifting a stray glass of wine, Caía asked, "Is this mine?"

"Phht," Marta replied, waving a hand in dismissal. "What does it matter? Soon we will be drinking from the bottle anyway." They were finishing number two, and ready for number three.

"So true," Caía said and proceeded to chug the last sip, then she wandered over to look into the pot that sat boiling on the stove. "So, what are these again?"

"Cañaíllas," Laura shouted.

The aroma was perhaps that of seafood, but the contents looked more like deformed escargot. "Are they sea snails?"

"No," said Marta. "More like conchas."

"Yummy, yummy for my tummy," Laura exclaimed. Using the phrase her uncle had taught her last night, she rubbed her belly with exaggerated circular motions. Really, Laura's grasp of the English language was far better than Caía would have supposed. With her too-big apron slightly askew, she held a wooden spoon in her right hand. "Can I spin them now, Mamá?" She danced, or more like wiggled. "Can I? Can I?"

"Can you stir them," Caía corrected her, but reluctantly, because in fact, she would be "spinning" them as well. The distinction scarcely held any merit, though she was bound to play the part of a dutiful English tutor, regardless that on any given day she felt more like a student. Even Laura had taught her so much about living in the moment.

Marta ignored her daughter's question as she sprinkled salt into the pot with a furrowed brow. "This is all you need, a bit of salt and maybe pepper. And, yes, you can make it spicy as well, but then my Laura will not like it too much."

"Yes! I do like too much," Laura corrected her mother, smacking her belly with the wooden spoon. "I do like it too much in my belly because they are yummy in my tummy!"

The child's excitement was inexhaustible.

"Yes," Marta said, turning to seize her daughter's spoon from her hand. She rapped Laura gently upon the head with it. "I know you like too much, chochete, but you will be sick if you eat too quickly as you did last time."

"I won't, Mamá. Te lo juro," Laura said, attempting to recapture her spoon. Each time she reached for it, Marta whisked it away. "Mamá," she cried.

"You won't do what?"

"I won't eat too much."

"Yes, because you must leave some for Caía, or she will go home and think you are rude."

At once, Laura shook her head. "Noooo, I don't want her to go," she said, glancing at Caía. The sentiment gave Caía an unexpected rush of joy.

"Very well, then you will be good," her mother said, handing the spoon back to Laura, and returning her attention to her boiling pot. "They are nearly done," she said. "Maybe two minutes more and we will take everything downstairs to the terraza and begin our fiesta de chicas. Sí?"

Girl's night in. It had been Caía's idea, and both Laura and Marta had thrilled over the prospect. On the table already, waiting to be hauled downstairs, were spiced olive oil with warm bread, cheese and jamón, and something called chicharrones.

Much of tonight's dinner appeared to come straight off a *Fear Factor* menu—at least for an unsophisticated Polish girl from Athens, Georgia. Admittedly, there were many things Caía had yet to eat, including escargot and raw oysters. Somehow, she'd reached the ripe old age of thirty-four without ever having swallowed a raw mollusk. However, she'd be darned if she'd let a five-year-old out *Fear Factor* her.

"Mira, Caía, I will teach you how to eat them," Laura said soberly. "They are easy for me now. Because I am big. When I was a baby, I couldn't do it."

"When were you ever a baby?"

Laura nodded, perhaps mistaking Caía's question, and Caía reached down, cupping Laura beneath the chin, holding her as she had done so many times to Jack. And just like Jack, Laura took the cue to rest her chin in the palm of Caía's hand. She smiled up at Caía, and Caía's heart ached.

How could she could lose her heart so easily to this child when it was still so full of grief over losing Jack?

Nobody could replace her son, but it felt great to be on the receiving end of Laura's trust. Little by little, Caía was finding her long-lost Zen. Maybe in part because Laura's uncle had decided to make himself scarce. For a little while every day, she could pretend Nicholas Kelly wasn't part of her life in the worst imaginable way. She wondered vaguely where he'd gone off to today.

Deeming the snails to be finished now, Marta hoisted the giant pot off the stove and carried it to the sink. "Quita," she said to her daughter. "Te voy a quemar." And Laura slid off the chair, out of her mother's way. With the pot safely over the sink, Marta strained the contents through a colander. And once that was done, she lifted the colander with the cañaíllas, and set it on a folded kitchen towel to catch excess water. Without segue, she asked, "Caía, do you know where the wine is? Ábreme otra botella, por favor."

"Another one?" Caía grinned. "We'll be fast asleep before eight."

"Maybe you, not me," Marta said with a kiss and a smile as she opened a cabinet and dragged out a blue porcelain bowl. "Here, we are more accustomed to our vino."

"Mami, that don't make sense. How can somebody be fast asleep?" Laura asked. "If people can be sleeping, they cannot be fast? They must be slow."

"It's just an expression," Caía explained as Marta dumped the contents of the colander into the bowl and Caía opened another bottle of wine.

By the time Caía handed Marta a full glass of wine, Laura was already onto something new. Standing on her chair again, she was blowing over the bowl full of cañaíllas, as though to cool them.

"Let me show you something," she said, picking out and holding up two small conches between her fingers. "Ow," she said, throwing one back down. But she nevertheless picked the same one up again, as though refusing to be defeated, but she frowned. "You have to be careful because they are hot. Mira," she said, holding up both conches for Caía to see.

Her mother turned around to watch, one hand on her hip, one hand cupped beneath the belly of her glass. "Do not cry si te quemas, Laura."

"I won't burn myself, Mamá. Look," she demanded again. "You have to take the pinchy part and poke it to the hole. Just like this." She demonstrated by sticking the pointy end of one conch into the shell of the other—a primitive-looking procedure. "And then you have to . . . pinch it out . . ." She did this swiftly, making it look simple. "And then you eat it." She popped the conch meat into her mouth and swallowed dramatically, before going back for more. "You can try now."

"Me cago en tu madre," Marta said testily, though she smiled at her daughter and took a sip from her wine glass as Caía accepted two small, relatively hot conches from Laura's hand.

Holy moly, the child must already have calluses on her fingers. As Laura had done, Caía tossed them down and picked them up again, and Laura squealed with laughter. Once she had them back in hand, she dug the pointy end of one conch into the shell of the other, trying to hook the meat and pull it out. In fact, she tried several more times, but every time, instead of hooking the conch meat, she shredded the edges.

Once more she tried, determined not to give up—especially after Laura picked up two more conches, and deshelled both before Caía could manage to do one.

"Looks like fun," Nick said, entering the room unexpectedly. He startled Caía. She flicked out the conch meat. It went flying behind her, smacking Nick Kelly on the left cheek. His reflexes were good; he caught the fruit of Caía's labors before it could fall to the floor.

Delighted, Laura shrieked again with laughter, and Marta laughed as well. Caía frowned—less at her foiled attempts and more because Nick was back.

"Welcome home, Nico," Marta said, waving him into the room, but he hesitated, giving Caía a sideways glance.

"We are having a fiesta de chicas, Tiíto Nick."

"Girls only? Or are boys welcome, too?"

The question was posed to Caía, and Marta watched their interaction curiously. "Of course," Caía said, peering down at her empty conch.

"There's a trick to that," Nick said, coming over and standing next to Caía. "May I?" He held his hand outstretched.

"I will go get you a cerveza, Tiíto," Laura said excitedly, rushing out of the room, down to the patio where they kept the beer. As boisterous as the child ran, by the time she returned, Caía was sure it would explode in Nick's face, and some part of her took guilty pleasure in that thought.

Marta turned her attention to the oven, pulling out the bread, and Caía was forced to accept Nick's help. She handed him both conches. Using the empty conch, he quickly hooked the pointy end into the thickest part of the meat, and ever so gently, dragged it out. "Want it?"

Caía shook her head and he answered with a grin. Without hesitation, and with a glint in his eye, he tossed the conch meat into his mouth.

❦

CHICAGO, TUESDAY, JUNE 14, 2016

Despite the back door opening and closing, Jack's nose remained firmly attached to his computer screen. Caía might have been a burglar for all he knew. Then again, he must realize burglars probably wouldn't park in their garage, which thereby narrowed the possible list of entrants to two, neither of which held much interest for him right now.

Teenagers—had she been so withdrawn? *No.* Because Caía didn't have parents who were always at each other's throats. She and Jack might share the distinction of being only children, but this was a fundamental difference between them, and it was formative. For Jack's sake, she and Gregg had called a truce, but things remained tense. Trust, once lost, was not easily regained.

Annoyed by the entire ordeal—by the complications her husband had introduced into their marriage—Caía set her purse and her keys on the counter and opened the fridge, wondering what to make for supper.

Gregg was supposed to have picked up her car from the shop, and since he didn't enjoy driving her car, Caía had been so sure he would come straight home. However, her car wasn't in its usual space out front. And of course, since Gregg insisted upon taking the garage, she'd pulled in, half expecting to find her car parked inside. The obvious conclusion now was that he wasn't home yet, and her stomach fluttered uneasily—not a sign of hunger, despite her foray into the fridge.

Remarkably, not even the open refrigerator distracted her son. She closed the door a little harder than she meant to. "Where's your dad, Jack?"

His response was full of indignation. "How should I know?"

Head low, he was bent over the kitchen desk, where Caía had moved his computer. A mauled bag of chips lay on the counter beside him, no doubt the reason he wasn't focused on dinner, and since Caía seemed to be good for little else these days, he didn't bother to turn and address her.

"Has he been home?"

"No."

Attitude. Caía considered ordering him to stop what he was doing and turn around to look her in the eyes when he was talking to her. But she didn't. Instead, hoping to remind him that whatever she felt about his dad, it didn't extend to him, Caía came up behind her son and placed a hand on his shoulder, the way she used to do when he was young. Back in the day, he might have turned and thrown his arms about her waist. Now, he sat stiffly, his shoulders tight, and the instant her hand lit upon his shoulder, it rose a full half-inch. But he didn't turn around.

"Maybe he went to the gym," he said, finally, reluctantly, and she could tell that he was uncomfortable with her proximity.

Caía moved away from the desk, leaning back against the island for support, giving Jack a bit of space. "I thought you said you didn't know where he was."

"He called to ask if you were home."

"And?" She was talking to his back.

"I said no."

"What else?"

"I don't know, Mom; he said he left his gym bag in his car."

Again, that uneasy feeling fluttered deep in Caía's gut.

True, the gym bag was in the trunk of his car—the car she was driving. Justified or not, the sight of it had given her a false sense of security. Because, of course, if he didn't have that goddamned gym bag, he couldn't go to the gym. *Right?*

Well, she didn't know why she would make such assumptions. He wasn't going to the gym to exercise anyway. It was only an excuse. "Did he say what time he'd be home?"

"Mom!" Jack turned to glare at her, his eyes glassy, as though he'd been crying.

The realization gave Caía an instant pang. Blinking, she swallowed her angry retort, realizing the position her son was in—the position Gregg had put him in. Because Jack wasn't stupid. And neither was she. Tears pricked at her own eyes and she turned away, returning to the fridge, opening the door again, staring blindly into the glass shelves, hoping to give Jack some sense of normalcy.

The shelves needed to be cleaned. Again. Used to be, she'd kept them spotless. Now she couldn't bring herself to care. It was a small thing, but one of many, many small things she was clearly neglecting.

If only she knew for sure.

What would she do?

Leave?

What about Jack?

What. About. Jack?

Tomorrow was his birthday and the mood in the house was funereal. The new skateboard beneath her bed would go a short ways toward making it up to him, but nothing was going to be normal until she and Gregg made some decisions.

Everything was fine, she told herself. Today was today and tomorrow was tomorrow. Jack was only thirteen. There would be plenty more birthdays to celebrate.

Anyway, he was a teenager now. If it wasn't this, it would be something else. She couldn't blame everything on Gregg, despite her wanting to.

Once again, Caía closed the refrigerator door and turned, grabbing an apple from the bowl on the island. On purpose, she left her purse—along with her cell phone—ignoring the little voice that demanded she grab her car keys and get back into her car and drive by the gym. If her car was parked there . . . if he'd gone to see that woman in her car . . .

Good God, she was sick of living this way—sick of suspicion and doubt. "I'll be upstairs," she said to Jack, biting into the apple with a vengeance.

It was as though she'd never spoken. Jack sat mutely at his computer, unwilling or unable to respond. And Caía had an inkling as to why. He, like Caía, knew exactly where his father was. Although they took care not to fight in his presence, he was bound to have overheard some of their arguments. She would like to have gone back to reassure him that none of this was his fault, but some part of her, like some part of him, wanted to pretend it didn't exist. And so she didn't, because vocalizing the truth only made it more real.

Get Jack, get in the car, and leave, a little voice in her head said. But a louder one prevailed. *You're tripping for no reason, Caía. He's probably on his way home right now. Get over it already. It's not like he doesn't know you know. If he wanted to leave, he would have already. Let it go.*

☙

JERÉZ, PRESENT DAY

"But, Tiíto, I want to because I need to say buenos días."
"You need to?"

Voices awoke Caía from a dreamless sleep. Her lids fluttered open, and her eyes focused on the dappled shadows dancing along her bedroom wall. Behind her, morning light filtered in through the window, muted by the leaves of the orange tree.

"Sí."

"No."

"But whyyyy, Tiíto Nick? Whyyyy?"

The sound was as plaintive as any sound Caía had ever heard. In this house, whispers tended to echo, but these were not whispers. Or rather, Nick's voice was low and his words softly spoken, but the words of a precocious five-year-old were not the least bit self-conscious.

"Because, Laura, not everyone gets up as early as you."

"But if I go to school and didn't get to say buenos días, she will cry." Her argument was adorable, if inherently flawed, and she sounded as though she were on the verge of crying herself.

It took Caía a full moment to realize they were speaking about her. Laura wanted to come in and wake her. Nick steadfastly refused to let her.

"She won't cry, Laura."

"Yes, she will. I promise, she will."

Silence.

"Tiíto . . . te lo juro."

"You promise what?"

"Que se va a llorar."

"What makes you think she will cry, Laura?"

"'Cause my mamá says Caía está triste, like we are. Los ángeles se llevaron a su hijo."

Because angels took her little boy. Caía's heart wrenched.

Silence.

Would Nick put two and two together? Had anyone ever mentioned this to him before? It didn't matter. She wasn't the only woman in the world who'd ever lost a child. He couldn't possibly know how Jack died. Not even Marta knew. Nobody knew anything, except what Caía had revealed. For all they knew, Jack might have been ill. Children died every day of one thing or another.

From the context of their dialogue, it appeared Nick was putting on her shoes and maybe tying her laces. "You want to try?"

"No. I can't do it," Laura said.

"Yes, you can," Nick argued. "All you have to do is make a loop . . . here, watch me."

"I don't want to wear them, Tiíto. I want to wear my tacones."

"No, Laura, your tacones are not for school," her uncle said quietly.

"¡Por favor!" she begged, and Caía rose to retrieve her robe, uncertain what exactly she meant to do. From the sound of their voices, she thought they must be seated in her salon—hers, as though she had any rights to any part of this house. She was a stranger, living here by the good graces of the house's mistress.

Except that Caía no longer felt like a stranger. She had begun to feel as though she belonged. Marta and Laura made her feel this way. Drawn by the conversation, she moved into the foyer of her room to eavesdrop.

"Well, I can take my abanico?"

The Spanish fan Caía had gifted her for her birthday. A tiny smile turned up the corners of Caía's lips. She was growing fond of that child and it wasn't difficult. She was adorably impetuous, but not in an obnoxious way. She simply was not the least bit shy about expressing her feelings. At any given moment, she said whatever she was thinking. Her mother and uncle both doted on her, and the effect of this was present in her attitude. Nick Kelly's influence was part of that child's well-being.

Caía wrapped her brain around that fact, moving into the breakfast nook to peer around the threshold. "Tiíto Nick" had positioned himself on one knee—like a man proposing—except that he was humbly tying the laces of a pair of red sneakers.

"You can have your abanico and your tacones when you get home, Laura."

Nick's tone was firm, not harsh, and Caía wondered if he'd ever wanted children of his own. He was gentle with Laura, and patient in a way Gregg had never been with Jack.

But then, Gregg never killed a child—at least not directly. She stared at the man on his knees, trying to picture him behind the wheel of his car . . . her son out in front of it.

"¡Por favor! Tiíto, I want to show my teacher."

Uncle Nick shook his head.

"Why not, Tiíto?" Laura asked, reaching out and touching her uncle's head gently, patting it lovingly. "¡Por favor!"

"You can win your way most days, minx, but not today. Today you will take your tiny butt to school, and when your teacher says it's time for show-and-tell, I will bring your abanico and your tacones another day."

Laura crossed her arms in protest, nevertheless allowing her uncle to continue lacing her shoes. Only now she straightened her back, looking for all the world like a princess who'd been denied her morning crumpet, chin up, pouty lips. "I will not like to leave them," she announced.

"I promise you will forget about them the instant you are with your friends."

"No, Tiíto," Laura argued. "I will not forget my beautiful tacones." And then her tone lifted, and she placed a finger to her chin, as though she had discovered a solution to please everyone. "Oh, but, Tiíto, listen to me . . . if you say yes, I can put my tacones and my abanico en el cuarto de Caía and she can take care of them for me, *vale*?" She thrust up a palm as though to say, "There? Are we happy now?"

Caía laughed quietly. Both Laura and her uncle looked up to catch her standing in the doorway. Caía pinched her robe together.

"Caía!" Laura shouted. She kicked her uncle's hand away, bounced up from the sofa, and ran to greet Caía, throwing her arms around Caía's legs. With a forbearing smile, her uncle let her go, but he remained on one knee, patiently holding Laura's remaining shoe. Automatically, Caía's hand moved to the child's head, hugging her awkwardly as her uncle watched.

"Caía, I want you to walk me to school."

"I am sure Ms. Nowakówna has better things to do," Nick said, but his eyes held a question . . . or perhaps a challenge?

The words rushed out before Caía could stop them. "Not really."

"Oh, yes," Laura exclaimed. "¡Por favor!" She turned to her uncle, seizing Caía by the hand and pulling with more vigor than a child of her age should have. "Tiíto," she said, "I only want Caía to take me, *vale*? Only for today. Not you." She shoved her palm out, as though to keep Nick at bay. "You can stay home, Tiíto Nick. Okay?"

There was no malice in the child's demand. Her voice held no resentment. But some mean part of Caía experienced a rush of satisfaction. It was quickly doused by the sight of Nick's genuine smile. "Caía may join us if she likes," he said, and there was a certain look in his eyes . . . a look that Caía couldn't quite define. It was as though he might be daring her.

"Well, I will have to get dressed first," she said. A glance at the clock on the wall revealed that there was more than ample time to make it to school and back before 9:00 a.m.

"We can wait," he said.

Their gazes held.

It came down to this: How badly did Caía wish to spend time with him? Or, more to the point: How badly did she want to know about her son's final moments? How easily could she bear this man's company in the pursuit of truth? No matter how "normal" being with Laura made her feel, this was what she had come for after all.

Besides, beyond what she might feel about Nick, Caía craved this tiny act of normalcy. It had been so very long since she'd walked any child to school—years and years and years, in fact. Toward the end, Jack had barely tolerated her driving him and letting him out at the curb. "You're wearing a robe," he'd said one day. "Mom." The single word held so much censure. Usually, it was "Ma" this, "Ma" that. Never "Mom," unless he was upset. But he didn't understand. How could he? Caía would never have told her thirteen-year-old son that she suspected his father was screwing a twenty-year-old from the gym. "No one will see," she'd said wearily.

Most days, she hadn't bothered to comb her hair. There was something debilitating about knowing one's husband was having an affair. Although maybe her response wasn't all that normal, because she knew other women who'd dressed a little nicer, wore more makeup, tried a little harder. Caía had disengaged, and she wasn't brave enough to make a change.

That morning—the morning of Jack's accident—if Caía could be honest with herself, it wasn't hurt or anger that had driven her to the Village Tap. It was curiosity.

Of course she was angry, but more than anger, she'd simply needed to know. She'd needed a kick in the ass to make a different decision.

"Caía?" Laura was looking up at her, wiggling her hand. "Do you want to take me to school?" she asked, her chocolate eyes wide, offering Caía another chance.

"Very much," Caía said, and her gaze slid to Nick. "I'll hurry," she promised.

"We'll be right here," he said.

※

It was a curious feeling to be walking the morning route, holding Laura's hand while Nick Kelly kept pace behind them. Today, not even his presence could dampen Caía's mood.

"Do you want to come into my class?" Laura asked.

"Maybe another day," Caía offered, and found she meant it. At least she wanted to mean it. She had intended to stay in Spain only long enough to learn what she needed to learn. But this very moment, she also wanted to be here long enough to visit Laura's class.

"*Vale*," Laura said.

It was the Spanish equivalent of "okay," and for the moment, everything was A-Okay. After a few weeks of being in that house with Laura and Marta, Caía could no longer think clearly about what it was she'd meant to say, or do, or what she hoped to accomplish by getting up-close-and-personal with Nick Kelly. Right now, he wasn't all that important.

What was important was the reality of Laura's hand in hers.

Focusing on the pleasure it gave her, Caía could even allow herself to tune out the sound of Nick's footsteps behind her, a constant reminder that at some point, she was bound to be discovered. But not today. Today was not the day to worry about consequences, not when she was experiencing the first moments of true joy she'd felt in so long.

Stranger yet was the simple fact that Nick Kelly was a part of this. He had allowed Caía to walk this child to school. He had given up his place at Laura's side, and even now he seemed content to remain in their shadow, one step behind.

They passed Rincon, and Caía peered over at the café, spotting her waiter. As usual, he was running around, sliding small plates onto café tables, and she realized only now that she'd never even asked him his name. *How rude.* She normally enjoyed chatting with people. When had she stopped doing that? The waiter caught her gaze and tilted Caía a familiar smile. Caía waved self-consciously, and didn't look to see if Nick noticed. If he should wonder about her familiarity with the waiter, or the café's proximity to their house, she didn't want him to ask. Not now.

The walk was over all too soon. By the time they stood in front of the doors leading into Laura's school, Caía was inexplicably reluctant to let her go inside. She fell to her haunches. "You have a beautiful day," she said, brushing a wayward strand from Laura's face.

Laura reciprocated, and then splayed both her sweet hands on Caía's cheeks. "Please, please walk me home after school today?"

She was always so very melodramatic. So full of passion for life. Caía wanted a little of that back. She glanced up at Laura's uncle. He was watching curiously, but said nothing, and Caía experienced a moment of dread. *This was it.* She would send Laura inside, and then she would have to make a choice. She could walk home with Nick—if that's where he was inclined to go—and tell him the truth, or she could beg off and say she had somewhere else to be.

Where?
Nowhere.
You're a coward.

Now was the time she should opt to face him, and Caía imagined herself asking him to grab a cup of coffee. They could go to Rincon—or somewhere else. Somewhere Caía had never been before, in case he made a scene. This could be her moment of truth, the moment she'd been waiting for . . .

Do you know who I am? her eyes pleaded.

With both her hands, Laura turned Caía's face again, forcing her to look at her, rather than at her looming uncle. Nick stood by quietly—not at all the sort of guy Caía had expected to find. Solemn, even cheerless at times. Except when he was speaking to his niece. "I can't," Caía said. "I have . . . something to do. But I will see you . . . when you come home, *vale?*"

For once, the child didn't press the issue. She nodded and Caía kissed her cheek, and stood. "Thanks," she said to Nick, not understanding why.

"See you later," he said, and Caía bolted away, in the opposite direction, toward the market where she and Marta had first met.

She didn't dare turn and look at him. She kept walking until she reached a quiet alley and then ducked inside. Right there, without any witnesses, Caía sat on a stoop and cried—for Jack. For the sense of betrayal she was feeling right now, for having spent a single minute not missing her son. For being who she was—a woman with too many secrets. *What are you doing?* she asked herself.

What are you doing, Caía?
What are you doing?
What the hell are you doing?

Eleven

Can I see another's grief, and
not seek for kind relief?
– *William Blake*

IT WAS TIME FOR A REDIRECT. Ambivalence where Nick Kelly was concerned wasn't getting Caía what she needed—whatever that was.

You don't belong here, Caía.

She had come for a reason, and now that she was here, so close to her goal, she was letting her emotions rule her. She was allowing some primitive yearning for fellowship intrude upon her primary objective. Okay, so maybe she didn't want to make Nick Kelly pay in some gruesome and unacceptable manner. But she did need him to look her in the face and tell her what in his life had been so damned important that he could allow himself to be distracted while sitting behind the wheel of his car. She needed him to see her—Jack's mother—and feel remorse.

She could easily firebomb everything right now. *Come clean.* But the truth was that once she confessed, all ties to Marta and Laura must be severed. They would look at her with something akin to horror. They might even call the police. Well, why wouldn't they? Caía wasn't who they thought she was. And, of course, she would have to move out. She would have to go home. Because home was where the heart was, after all. *Right?*

But what if the heart were nowhere? Unanchored by people or places. Given this lens, it shouldn't seem so crazy for someone to leave everything behind and set out searching for answers. Wasn't this the impetus for discovery? Marco Polo went searching for spices. David Livingstone went in search of the Nile. Leif Ericson—well, he simply got lost, but in each of these cases, Caía was certain there was nothing keeping these explorers at home, and there was one powerful motivator luring them away: the pursuit of truth. In the end, neither spices nor rivers were Caía's objective, but if reasons were subjects in the land of rationale, truth must be king.

Don't get distracted, Caía.
Don't let your heart trip you up.
If you do, all will be lost.

Before Jack was born, Caía had dreamt of traveling the world. Even after marrying Gregg, she had envisioned the two of them traveling together. Gregg, on the other hand, had never had the first inkling to leave Athens—not even after he got the job offer in Chicago. It was Caía who had talked him into it, and at the time, she'd accused him of having no sense of adventure.

He, on the other hand, accused Caía of having a wandering heart. He'd asked why she couldn't be content to stay at home, with him—the irony being that she would have remained faithful until her dying breath while Gregg got going the instant the going got tough.

But that was no longer here nor there. What Caía was coming to realize was that she, unlike Gregg, had shallow roots. Gregg's ancestors had fought in the Civil War. He owned a rifle that once belonged to Jefferson Davis. His second cousin in Atlanta once worked in *the* drug store where Coca-Cola was invented, where they sold the hangover remedy for five cents a glass. Gregg was content in Athens, and in the end, Caía was certain he'd grown resentful that she'd pressed him into moving away. They were not the same, she and he. Caía had always understood, deep down, that once her parents were gone, she would be as unfettered as a dandelion seed. All that had presumably changed with Jack. Once her son was born, Caía had felt . . . anchored. And when he died . . . *Poof.* One good puff, and like a dandelion seed, up, up and away she went.

Except, she was gone before that. Physically, she had remained there, on that couch in Roscoe Village, with her notebook on her lap . . . surfing and daydreaming about another life.

What if she could finish her language studies? What if she could get a job in Washington? Or anywhere, really. She didn't need to hold any highfalutin job. Caía just wanted something more out of life than what she had—a husband who spent more hours away than he did at home, and a son who didn't appreciate the sacrifices Caía made.

Meanwhile, two blocks north, in his perfectly restored brownstone, lived the man who would run down her world. *Literally.*

Of course, they hadn't known each other then. In a neighborhood with more than thirty thousand people, it was impossible to know, much less recognize all your neighbors.

Caía wanted to hate Nick Kelly. But it was difficult to watch him with Laura and not see a different man. She needed to think of him as a monster, but it wasn't the case. He was only a man. A man who had given up a successful partnership in Chicago to come help his sister-in-law and niece transition through his brother's death. For all the things Caía had heard about him back home, all the things she'd witnessed here in Spain declared something else.

While everyone was out, she slipped into Nick's room, snooping to see how he lived. While there was little doubt his quarters in this house were grand, it was just a bedroom in a house, no different from Caía's suite downstairs—or rather, hers was nicer. But neither room compared to the five-thousand-square-foot brownstone he'd sold in Roscoe Village, a house that had listed and sold for nearly two million dollars. Essentially, Nick had given up everything to come live like a teenager in his mother's house. Except that, instead of sitting around playing video games all day long, he cared for his niece, giving her his undivided attention, and maybe even forsaking his own chances for a family in the interim. Put so bluntly, it made him seem like a saint . . . a saint who'd just happened to kill her son.

Nothing made sense anymore.

Caía's brain was incapable of filtering through what was logical and what was not logical. But one thing she realized . . . her presence in this house was not normal. It was not logical. Lines were being blurred—and crossed.

And those weren't the only lines blurring. Caía noticed, more and more, that rather than teach Laura proper English, she more often lapsed into Spanish, insinuating herself into their routines. And contrary to what she may have believed, it wasn't making her feel worse. Bewildered by this fact, she peered up at the stars.

Tonight, the wind was brisk. It carried a mean chill, but in the shelter of the patio, it was still nice. Nevertheless, seated where she was, there was a limited view of the night sky.

The jardín was enclosed by vine-covered stucco walls that were easily thirty feet high. Along the edges were small raised gardens with miniature roses.

The house itself was like a storybook palace, and there was even an ancient well in the center of the yard, flanked by citrus trees—one lemon, one orange. The orange tree sat outside her bedroom window. She stared hard at the well, imagining the hands that built it. Having gone without rain for so long, the scent of water was absent here, but Caía could easily picture servants standing next to it, hauling up buckets to fill the upstairs baths. Quite likely, that well had been there since before both world wars, and that woman upstairs—the one who'd never once suspected Caía of anything—was related to the people who'd built it, or rather, who'd had it built, as the case must be. Marta couldn't help it; she had a genteel demeanor that had no doubt taken her family centuries to ingrain. Even her grief was more refined, while Caía's was raw and festering, like a leper whose wounds couldn't heal.

And Caía's biggest fear of all: What if her heart were damaged beyond repair? What if this was who she was now? *Cold, deep down.*

Rather than start a fire in the brazier, Caía borrowed a blanket from her bedroom, because despite Marta's insistence that she should treat this house as her own, Caía couldn't make the leap from guest to resident, and so, of course, she would never really consider herself a member of this family, no matter how long she stayed . . . no matter how much she insinuated herself into their lives. And once this was all over, where was home?

Not Chicago. As fabulous as that city was, Caía had never belonged there. And yet, even in Athens, where she had grown up, Caía never really felt as though she'd belonged there either. Her parents had worked hard to build a comfortable home in a quiet neighborhood, but as a family, they had been like fish out of water.

For the most part, growing up, Caía's mother and father had kept to themselves, stoic and silent. Their joy was entirely invested in Caía, and even though Caía made a few good friends in Athens, her parents weren't the type to reach out to other parents, or drink margaritas on the deck. For her dad, game day beers in a cooler held no appeal. He worked hard every day, and came home to put his love and support into his family. Her mother had been his world and, as their only child, Caía had been the light of her parents' lives. So, when Jack and both her parents died, so too did her roots.

Admittedly, Caía had never had the same sense of familiarity with Gregg, but she understood now that she was probably equally responsible for that. In fact, only now did she understand that she had married Gregg for all the wrong reasons—to have a family. Jack had been her one true anchor. And once her son was gone, she might have kept trying, except Gregg wasn't equipped for that. He too had married Caía for all the wrong reasons—because it was the thing to do. Not the right thing. Just the thing. Because they'd dated all throughout high school and because they'd had sex in his parents' car. And also because his dad gave him "the talk." "Keep your dick in your pants, son, 'less you plan to put a ring on her finger, hear me?"

Well, Gregg did that . . . and once he took the dick out of his pants and put the ring on her finger, the romance was gone. No more sex in cars. No more sex in their bedroom either—at least not often. And then he'd gone and put his dick, again, where it didn't belong.

Caía didn't care anymore, but that didn't mean she wasn't still furious with him. Not because he'd cheated, but because instead of dealing with his own sense of loss—with Caía and her grief—he'd shut her out. Throwing away all their years together, he'd left her when she'd needed him most, pushed her off into other people's hands—like unwanted things. *Castaways. Worthless trash.*

The hospital had been a short-term stay, but the house was already empty when they let Caía go home. Picked clean of everything he'd valued. Caía imagined he'd set up a new house somewhere else. It all seemed so strange now, she realized. Marta would certainly think she was crazy. Nick would think she was mad. Laura wouldn't understand . . .

"Penny for your thoughts?"

Startled by Nick's voice, Caía squealed in surprise.

"Sorry about that," he said, and automatically Caía hoisted up the blanket like a shield. *Don't give him a reason to suspect you.* She forced herself to look at him standing in the threshold of the door. She'd left both the door and the iron gate open, because she'd been afraid to lock herself out. The keys were inside, on the desk, but Caía didn't feel entitled to carry them around.

Leaning into the threshold on one shoulder, her would-be demon dangled a Cruzcampo from one hand, his fingers toying with the ridges around the bottle's lip.

"I haven't heard that phrase in years," Caía said, trying to be casual despite the pounding in her heart. She hadn't spoken to Nick since the morning she'd left him and Laura at the schoolhouse door. "I was thinking about . . . home . . ."

Averting her gaze, Caía peered up at the stars, wondering what brought him downstairs at such a late hour. Like Marta's, his room was upstairs, both at opposite ends of the long hall. Laura's room was next to her mother's. Caía's was the only one downstairs. There was nothing he needed down here—except maybe his beer.

At first, Caía had thought Nick must be banging his brother's wife—because wasn't that what men did? Bang women? But she saw no signs of that—no flirtation at all. In fact, Marta appeared to have set her matchmaking sights on Nick and Caía, attempting to place them together at every turn. Maybe this was why she'd so readily adopted Caía?

All week long, Caía had remained downstairs, taking rainchecks for dinners, and even Laura's joyful laughter hadn't lured her upstairs. She was afraid now . . . terrified of what she might say or do. But this couldn't go on forever. It simply couldn't. At some point, she had to come clean—or not—but one way or the other, she had to go.

Cicadas hummed on the power lines, the sound as frenetic as octave scales on a violin. It wound Caía's nerves. All the while, Nick stood, looking at her, and he finally asked, "So where's home?"

Caía didn't want to tell him.

But then again, this could be the perfect opportunity to learn a thing or two about the man she'd come four thousand miles to face. Maybe then she could leave in peace?

So here she was . . .

And there he was . . .

Caía lifted her blanket, tossing it up and over her left shoulder. "That's the point, I guess . . . I don't know where home is . . . not anymore."

With the beer in his right hand, he indicated the patio chair facing her. "Mind if I sit?"

"No. Of course not."

Why did he have to be so damned polite?

He moved out of the doorway and sat in the chair facing Caía—so close their knees might have brushed—except that Caía took care not to allow it. She moved her legs aside, and the gesture brought a twisted smile to Nick's lips. He tipped his beer up, throttling the neck of his bottle as he drank and then stopped and looked at her. "So . . . are you settled yet?"

Caía frowned, disoriented.

He swept the butt of his beer in an arc about him. "I mean the house."

"I suppose." Caía hugged herself, peering down at the blanket in her lap as his gaze examined the garden, sweeping the entire circumference of the yard. She plucked at a thread.

"You should have seen this place before Jimmy got hold of it," he said conversationally, and the admiration in his tone was so evident. Caía listened, letting him fill the silence, not trusting herself to speak.

Maybe in a minute. Maybe then she would say everything she'd come all this way to say. Maybe if she sat quietly, she might work up the nerve.

He pointed at the wall at the opposite end of the garden. "Her father bought that house next door, but Marta sold it to pay for repairs." *Silence.* "Jimmy designed the garden," he said, rambling a bit. "He wanted it to be like a paradise for his daughter—the lemon tree . . . the roses." He glanced at the well. "They put safety bars over that well, but the structure is original to the house." He pointed to the well with his bottle, which was already half empty, Caía noticed.

She nodded, and once again they lapsed into silence as she looked around at everything except Nick's face. He made her uncomfortable for reasons that went far beyond her son's death. Nicholas Kelly was an unknown commodity.

He'd chosen a seat untouched by moonlight, but Caía could sense, even through the darkness, that his eyes were fixed on her. *As it seemed they had been all week long.* It took every bit of her resolve to keep from looking him straight in the eyes and asking, "Why did you kill my son?"

"Caía . . ."

She met his gaze. "Yeah?"

"Have I done something to offend you?"

Caía's throat tightened. She shook her head, feeling ambushed. She hadn't yet figured out how to broach the truth, what words to say. "I don't know . . . maybe it's the divorce."

He seemed to consider her answer a moment, moving slightly forward so that moonlight revealed his chin and lips. "I take it you didn't want it?"

"No, no, that's not it," Caía said, but she didn't elaborate.

"What then?"

She hugged herself, feeling shivers coming on. Like an injured body in shock. *How long before Jack's body shut down. The doctors said death was instantaneous, but how could they really know?*

He suddenly got up, and Caía hoped he was leaving, but instead he walked over to the small built-in fridge beneath the tiled counter, across the patio, and opened it, taking out another Cruzcampo. He set the old bottle on the counter and turned to ask, "Want one?"

Fabulous. Wonderful. Go on, Caía, pour fuel on the fire, she mocked herself, but said, "Why not." *Weak*, she berated herself as he picked up another beer and he opened both bottles against the edge of the counter. Then he came over and handed one to Caía before sitting again, facing her as he sipped thoughtfully at his beer.

Caía caught a whiff of alcohol-laced sweat, and wondered how long he'd been drinking today. She didn't remember any abundance of bottles in the trash, or evidence of alcohol in his room. And yet, that scent he had, while not offensive, meant he had been drinking long enough for it to work its way to his pores. Caía raised her beer. "How many have you had?"

His eyes glinted in the moonlight. "A few."

A few, as in "just a few"? Or a few, as in "more than a few"? Caía considered this as she took a slow, thoughtful sip of her own beer. The sound of cicadas grew in frequency, and she braced herself as some sixth sense warned her to go inside.

Go to bed. Tomorrow's another day.

Nick was silent a long, long while, and Caía got the impression he was trying to find the nerve, or perhaps the words to say something out loud. "I hope you don't mind," he said finally. "Marta told me . . . everything."

Caía's gaze snapped to his face. She blinked. "Everything?"

"About your son."

"Oh." Frowning, Caía wrapped her hands about her bottle's neck, concentrating on the cold bottle sweat. Her shivers intensified, completely out of proportion with the night's temperature. And now there was an elusive scent in the air, one that tasted a lot like fear.

"You don't need to talk about it if you don't want to," he said, pulling down another long sip and sinking further into his wicker chair. "We all have demons," he said, out of context.

And you are mine.

But maybe he wasn't talking out of context. Maybe he thought Caía was somehow responsible for Jack's death. "I have nothing to feel guilty about," she said defensively.

"I'm sorry, I didn't mean to imply." His lips turned a bit derisively. "I guess I was referring more to myself."

Caía stiffened. The universe seemed to be handing her the perfect opportunity to come clean—right here and now—to look Nick Kelly in the eyes and ask him about her son.

I know what you did, she said silently. But her lips wouldn't part to speak.

For the longest interval, he sat nursing his beer, and Caía hoped that this was where he would leave it. If they didn't clear the air tonight, she would make her plans to leave. If she couldn't take this optimal moment, and ask him what she needed to ask him, then it was surely time to go.

But what was funny, she realized, was that it wasn't Nick she was afraid of. It was herself. The image of her own bloodied face in the bathroom mirror flashed through her mind, and she sat quietly, shivering on the sofa.

She hadn't really thought about what might happen in that moment. She had merely reacted in fury and in pain. And when she thought about it now, really thought about it, she must have hurled herself over that sink, because normally a person couldn't easily smack their head on a bathroom mirror. But Caía didn't remember much about it. Later, at the hospital, the doctors had plucked glass shards out of her hairline, as though she'd rammed into that mirror like an angry bull. It was crazy any way you looked at it. As was this . . .

After another moment, Nick shook his beer, and finding it empty, he got up to procure another. Without a word, he plucked a bottle from the fridge, popped the top on the counter, this time without asking Caía if she wanted another, and he came back to sit down.

Caía pulled her blanket around herself, building a cocoon, sipping at her beer. The tension in the air was palpable. The house itself remained quiet, and Caía imagined both Marta and her daughter had already gone to bed. Inside, the streaming of the fountain was a constant white noise. And then suddenly, like a volcano that had remained dormant far too long, Nick's confession oozed out. "I killed a boy," he said, almost too softly to be heard.

But Caía heard and froze. Her throat narrowed, preventing words from escaping. He tapped his Cruzcampo on the arm of his chair, and said, "I didn't mean to."

Caía sought his eyes in the darkness and found them glistening.

"He was just a kid," he said, staring at his lap. "He had his whole life ahead of him."

It was too much to bear. Caía was both terrified to hear any more and terrified he might stop. She swallowed hard, and dared to ask, "H-how?"

"Car accident." He shook his head, as though he wished to deny the existence of his own memories. "I was on the way home from work . . . he was . . ." He twisted his neck, as though the tension there was painful. "... on a skateboard... my phone rang."

Beneath the blanket, Caía joined her hands prayerfully, trying to stop the tremors. She balled her hands into fists, resisting the urge to fly at him, as she'd always imagined she would do. Scratch out his eyes, rail at him, *why, why, why?*

"I didn't answer it. I wouldn't have. But I did turn away... just for a second." He sat up, leaning forward, moonlight illuminating his entire face now. Cradling his beer between his legs, he sat staring at the patio tiles, avoiding Caía's gaze. "I swear to God," he said. "It was just a split second."

Hot tears filled Caía's eyes. "What then?" she heard herself ask, and her voice was raw and scratchy with emotion.

He shrugged, meeting Caía's gaze, and Caía was stunned to find his eyes filled with tears. The sight of them left her confused. He seemed in that instant to be nearly as tormented by Jack's death as she was. "The road was clear... and next thing I knew..." He closed his eyes and a long, awkward silence followed.

Oh, God. What if, in fact, it was an accident? Unavoidable by its definition. What if he had been driving to the best of his ability? What if there was a good reason the police never charged him? What if her son was at fault?

No. It was the world's duty to safeguard the young. Caía couldn't fathom any God—if there was a God—who could forsake the innocent.

She didn't know what to say, or how to say it. She couldn't bring herself to comfort Nick—only how did you loathe a man who sat there crying over your son? *Real tears.*

Gregg must have cried as well, though Caía never witnessed it.

At first, maybe because he had been trying to be strong for her, and then later, he just never did. Only now, after everything was said and done, Caía couldn't say for sure whether Gregg was as torn apart by Jack's death as she was. *As Nick Kelly appeared to be.* Some part of Caía wanted to beg him to go on . . . to tell her what he saw that day—right down to the smallest detail—but she didn't have the strength of heart to hear more words coming out of his mouth.

Did he realize who she was?

Their gazes held, and Caía didn't think so. There was nothing staged about his confession. He genuinely seemed to need to unburden himself, and the simple fact that Caía was the last person on Earth he should be doing this with, was lost to him.

And then something unexpected happened.

Caía searched her heart. She couldn't find the loathing she'd expected to feel over Nick's confession—loathing she had nursed. In fact, she'd tended her anger like a rare and precious flower. Inexplicably, it was tired and wilted. And in its place grew a heavy, heavy sorrow.

Still, some part of her refused to part with her anger . . .

Because anger wasn't as debilitating as grief. She struggled for something to say. "There have been times when I've left my house and arrived at my destination without ever remembering the journey in between. Maybe you were distracted?"

His brows collided. "No," he said, crossly. And it was then Caía realized how leading her question must have sounded. "It was only a split second," he said defensively, his gaze piercing her through the shadows. "That was all it took." He shook his head, and chugged another sip of his beer. "Hey, look, I'm sorry, Caía. I don't know why I felt compelled to tell you any of this." He swept a thumb beneath each of his eyes. "I'm sorry."

"No . . . don't apologize," Caía said.

Unexpectedly, his anger turned inward. "I keep thinking any day now they're going to come lock me up, and it's probably exactly what I deserve."

"They didn't charge you."

It wasn't a question, but he didn't seem to notice.

"No."

Tears formed in Caía's eyes. "Some prisons you carry with you," she said quietly.

"I suppose," he said. And then, "I know it's not fair, but I feel like I lost that kid myself. I can't explain it, Caía. Before that accident, I didn't know anything about him... where he was going... all I knew was in those last seconds, that kid looked at me as though he wanted me to tell him everything was going to be all right. Less than one second later—just one tiny second—I saw the light leave his eyes, and I realized... nothing was ever going to be all right."

A dam burst in Caía's soul.

Nothing about this meeting had gone as she had anticipated. Tears flowed down her cheeks, unchecked. Sobs burst from her lips. She lifted her hands to her face and wept openly in front of the man who'd killed her son. She could hear him weeping as well, and they wept together.

They were alone on the patio. Nick reached out and touched Caía's cheek with the back of his knuckles, wetting them with her tears. Instinctively, Caía leaned into the caress, and suddenly he took Caía by the hand, pulling her into his arms.

Caía went without a word, clinging to the one person in the world she felt connected to right now. Connected by Jack, by his death. Before this instant, there had been no physical attraction between them—none that she could have put into words. But death had a power beyond imagining, and Caía had a hole in her heart.

She wrapped her arms around Nick's waist, and did something she never imagined she might do. She pressed her lips against Nick Kelly's mouth, weeping softly, and tearing a guttural moan from his lips. She tasted the salt of his tears, he lapped up hers . . . until it was impossible to distinguish whose grief she was tasting.

Like her son's accident, this too happened fast. One minute, they were grieving together, and the next they were groping one another out in the shadows of the patio. Warm hands on cold skin, touching her where no one had touched Caía in years. Tongues mingling. She tasted alcohol . . . and tears. Their kissing grew fevered. Nick's hand reached down, cupping her crotch with an open palm, giving her every chance to say no.

But she didn't say no. Instead, Caía reached down, pressing his fingers tighter against her, letting her body come to life. She pressed her nipples against his warm chest, her lips against his throat, biting him punitively, and then curatively. And then, the next minute, he lifted Caía up and carried her into the house, making a sharp left toward Caía's room, never breaking the kiss.

Sex was life-affirming. Death was final. Pleasure was a beacon in the darkness.

Twelve

All that we love deeply
becomes a part of us.
– *Helen Keller*

"COFFEE?"

Nick's voice stopped Caía as she reached for her purse. She turned to face him, shocked to find that "no" was not the first answer that popped into her head. "I thought you were already gone," she said.

"Marta took Laura to school this morning. Parent-teacher meeting—I think."

Sex was one thing, but Caía considered an actual conversation over coffee—with Nick. The thought was both terrifying and tempting all at once. This is what she'd come for, after all, except that last night's . . . whatever you wanted to call it—slip—had put her in a strange place. It couldn't happen again. It shouldn't have happened the first time, but it did.

There was no doubt Nick had been deeply affected by her son's death, and this bonded them in a way Caía might never have foreseen . . . but to sit there, talking to him one on one across a hot, steaming cup of coffee like nothing ever happened seemed ill conceived.

And yet . . . how did you sleep with a man you weren't willing to share a coffee with? She swung her purse over her shoulder. "Sure . . . sounds great." But she had a hard time looking him in the face. "Did you have a place in mind?"

"As a matter of fact, I do." They stood for a moment, awkwardly facing one another, and probably in the instant when he might have taken her by the hand—like a normal couple might have done—he inclined his head toward the door and said, "After you."

Caía bolted for the door, before she could change her mind. Outside, there was a surreal quality to the day. The sky seemed entirely too blue. Birds flitted to and from the balcony to the maple tree's branches and then back again, chirping merrily. In general, colors appeared brighter. There was a sweet scent in the air, not unlike the scent of oranges, but more like pollen.

"This way," Nick said, glancing at Caía's left hand.

Caía shoved both hands into her pockets, following slightly behind.

As it turned out, he didn't lead her very far, just across the street.

"Inside or out?" he asked.

"Inside," she said, but mostly because she felt odd about having witnesses to their date—or rather, it was only coffee. *It wasn't a date.* Anyone would think it was perfectly normal to see them together at a coffee shop across the street. After all, they lived under the same roof, and . . . last night . . .

Don't think about that.

Inside, the café was empty. Nick pointed to a two-seater table, leaving Caía to settle in as he moved toward the counter, launching into a conversation with the proprietor, a quiet, balding gentleman who seemed to take his coffee quite seriously, judging by the look on his face as Nick rattled off his order. In fact, they had a lengthy discussion about coffee as Caía eavesdropped—something about showing "the guiri" how to order.

"Here you go; time for a lesson," Nick said, returning with two small white cups in his hands. He set both cups down on the table, clinking them together, somehow managing not to spill a single drop.

"A lesson?"

He grinned. "About coffee."

Caía rolled her eyes. "I know coffee."

Nick shook his head adamantly. "Not judging by the coffee you drink. So here, this is the deal," he said, sliding into his chair. "You and I"—he pointed to her, and then to himself—"we're what's known here as guiris."

"Guiris?"

"Foreigners."

"Yeah?"

"Yep. So, if you"—he pointed to Caía—"order a café con leche, they'll assume you're a wuss and you're going to get some weak-ass coffee with these packets of sugar." He lifted one of the small, elongated red-and-white packets on the saucer and shook it.

Caía had never seen him so animated, except with Laura. "So?"

"So? I ask you: Do you want coffee with your milk? Or do you want milk with your coffee?"

Caía lifted a brow. "What's the difference?"

"Funny you should ask." He pushed one cup across the table to her, and Caía accepted it, wrapping her hands around the offering and pulling it close, warming her hands by the heat of it.

The scent was strong, surprising her with the rich aroma, and Caía brought the cup to her lips, surprised again to find the taste was equally pleasant.

"That is café cortado," he explained.

"Café cortado?"

"Coffee cut with a bit of milk."

"Um, really, what's the difference?"

"The taste," he said, with a French flair of his hand. Caía laughed over the silliness of his gesture. "No, really."

"Really," he insisted. "It's the taste. What you're drinking is basically a café solo with a dab of milk. What you normally drink, on the other hand, is what's known by true coffee drinkers as café manchada, which is more like a little coffee with a lot of milk."

Caía laughed again. "I see."

"Then, of course, you always have the option of asking for a descafeinado. But beware—ask for descafeinado de maquina, unless you want crappy instant coffee poured into a cup of hot milk."

"Sounds complicated," Caía said.

"Life is complicated," he shot back.

"You're telling me."

Nick took a sip from his own coffee and winked at her. "I really needed this after last night."

"Hungover?"

"A little. And I suppose I should apologize, but I don't want to."

He grinned, and so did Caía.

"Then don't."

"Okay, I won't."

Caía inhaled sharply as he peered at her over the rim of his little white cup.

"In all seriousness, do you . . . have regrets?"

Caía thought about his question for less than a moment, surprised to find she didn't. Or rather, she did, but not about anything that happened between them last night.

"So, you never explained, 'why Spain?'"

Caía smiled. "Yes, I did, but maybe you didn't like my answer? I told you the first day I met you that it seemed as good a place as any to recover from my divorce."

"The first day?" He seemed to think about it a moment, and nodded. "So, no friends here, right?" He sipped from his cup, once again studying Caía over the rim.

Caía shook her head, uneasy about the direction of their conversation.

"No family?"

"Nope," she said, defiantly. Plenty of people visited places without familial relationships. What should that prove?

Nick smiled then, setting down his cup. "Do you believe in fate, Caía?"

Caía toyed with the handle of her cup, turning it slightly. "I don't know." She looked at him warily. "Do you?"

Nick shrugged. "I think every action we choose has consequences. But no, I don't believe in fate, per se. However, I think sometimes we're drawn, like magnets, to people with . . . let's say, like minds. For example, what made you and Marta connect that day in the market?"

You.

The single word teetered on the edge of Caía's tongue. She took a slow purposeful sip from her coffee cup and peered up over the rim, into Nick's eyes, feeling as though the question wasn't random. Could he have finally realized who she was?

But no, rather, she had the sense that maybe he was testing her somehow. There was only one way he could know who she was and that was if he had pried in her room—snooped through her iPad. Even then, it wasn't certain he would make the connection, because Caía didn't have the same last name as Jack. She certainly wrote it that way while she and Gregg were married, but legally, she'd never changed her maiden name. She was glad now, because she didn't have any more tethers to Gregg. At any rate, what sort of a name was Paine?

Paine. Pain. It was as though she'd been destined for heartache with that name. Lindsey was welcome to it—and to Gregg. She hoped the two of them would be happy together. She didn't miss that man, and as much as she'd believed she'd hated the guy sitting in front of her, she was more connected to him than she'd ever felt with Gregg.

Caía wanted to tell Nick the truth, but to what purpose? Who would it serve? "I don't know. We just . . . bumped into each other."

"Literally? Like you ran into each other, spilled your produce, and decided to live happily ever after?"

Just like that? Did he believe that choosing to be happy was a simple decision? "Not exactly. I was going to buy some fish, and I wanted to know why Marta walked away from one of the vendors."

"And did she tell you?"

"No."

Nick watched her. "It might have been Jose Luis. He's the younger brother of—well, someone Marta dated before she married my brother. His brother handed off the business, but Marta, for some reason, keeps going there. Maybe hoping to see him. I don't think Jose Luis intends for that to happen."

"They did seem a bit at odds."

"I'm sure they were. After Jimmy died, Jose Luis asked Marta out—talk about making things complicated. She wasn't ready, and I'm guessing he took it personally. Although, I don't think she had any interest in him . . . more his brother."

"Yeah, well . . . it happens."

"Hope you don't mind if I ask . . . is your divorce final?"

"All but the crying," Caía joked.

His tone was sober. "And . . . are you crying?"

Not about that.

Caía shook her head. This was the one thing she knew for certain. Gregg was out of her life—especially now that there was no child to keep them together.

"Good," Nick said, and he lifted his cup in a toast. "Whatever the reason, I'm glad you picked Spain. Here's to new beginnings, Caía. ¡Viva españa!

Caía hesitated a moment, and then lifted her cup as well, tinkling it softly against Nick's. But she didn't return the toast, knowing intuitively that this was the beginning of the end—a thought that left her feeling hollow in a way she didn't expect.

≈

Seated in the tub, surrounded by flickering candles, Caía tried to remember a time when joy was her drug of choice, because yes, emotions were like drugs. Anger was a drug. *Sadness. Drug.* People got addicted to their pain. For Caía, it was the anger she'd latched onto, gripping it like a stiff-necked bulldog between locked jaws, allowing it to infuse her with a sense of purpose.

Now . . . something was happening.

She'd begun to wean herself off the anger, resuscitating pleasure in small shocks, like tiny, new blips on a flatlined monitor.

The taste of food, the sound of a child's laughter, quiet moments of friendship . . . these were small events that worked like defibrillators, shocking her senses back to life.

But it was Marta who'd opened that door for her, literally and figuratively. Along with Laura. And Nick. Like some cosmic event—grief particles floating around in the atmosphere—Caía had been drawn to these people like ions to an energy field.

She was teetering on the edge of a precipice. Tip one way, and she might topple in and never find her way back out of the abyss.

Or she could make a different decision . . .

Like you ran into each other, spilled your produce, and decided to live happily ever after?

To let it go, or not to let it go . . . this was the question—at least for Caía. If she allowed herself to do this, she might find her way back . . .

Certainly, there were things she could latch onto here, living in the lap of luxury.

For one, this was a grand old tub. She picked up a bar of soap—a lemony wedge that produced deep, rich suds. The scent encouraged her to inhale deeply, fill her lungs. She ran the wedge over her skin, pausing between her breasts, sliding it down between her thighs.

Ah, yes, soap was delightful . . .

Sex was too . . . even when it shouldn't be happening.

Or maybe it was better because it shouldn't be happening? *Taboo, and all that.*

Caía pried her mind off the man lying upstairs, probably in bed by now, probably fast asleep. She craved something, but not revenge, not satisfaction, not love—no . . . this was something entirely primitive. She felt an addiction simmering in her veins, driving her to get up out of the tub. Even now, enveloped by the warmth of the water, it was the heat of his skin calling out to her.

Don't think about that.

Pizza, she thought. Pizza could be sensational—Chicago deep dish. Not that Pizza House variety, with all the gooey cheese that wasn't even real.

That last night with Jack, when Gregg was "working late," she'd sold him on a pizza pie, heaped high with anchovies.

So they went to that place on North Clark Street, the one he liked so well, and Caía ordered the biggest pizza they had, topped with a double order of anchovies.

Well, as it turned out, her son didn't love anchovies. Annoyed, Caía had plucked them all off, knowing Jack was likely to eat most of it. And that was fine, she had reassured herself, because it meant she could have the anchovies to herself. Really, not very hungry, she'd placed them one by one in a dish and set them aside, intending to pile them onto her own slice—if there was any left when she returned from the restroom. But the dish was gone when she sat down again, and rather than order more, she'd sat nursing her disappointment—in fact, she'd mourned the loss of those anchovies as much as she'd mourned the loss of her marriage. She'd had herself a good little pity party over it, and all the while Jack sat across the table, long faced because he'd forgotten to tell the waiter to leave her dish of anchovies.

But that was the trouble with expectations; so often they led to disappointment. Caía had expected her marriage to fulfill her. She'd expected life in Chicago to be exciting. She'd expected her son to love all the things she loved simply because Caía had loved them.

But you didn't not eat a pizza simply because there were no anchovies on it. So, they ate the damned pizza, and Caía loved it. After all, it was perfectly reasonable to enjoy pizza without anchovies. Seeing her son's long face, she'd made a conscious decision not to begrudge the loss of those anchovies, and the instant she'd let it go, Jack's smile returned.

When you got right down to it, loss could be a bit like that pizza pie with anchovies. Simply because they'd been plucked away didn't mean they didn't linger still.

"That was the best pizza I ever ate, Ma," he'd said, licking his fingers. He was digging under his nails, and Caía didn't have the heart to tell him to stop. The smile on his face was too wonderful.

Caía sighed longingly. It was the best pizza Caía had ever eaten as well, though not because of anything that was on or off it. She'd spent that entire evening with her son—never worrying about Gregg or what he might be doing. It was just the two of them, mom and son, smack dab in the middle of the moment, and for a while, no one was angry or disappointed about anything at all.

Reaching out with a foot, Caía wrapped her toes around the faucet dial, turning on the water, refilling the tub with warm water, albeit feeling guilty over the rush of noise. Except for the running water, the house was still, and the water seemed to play in stereo.

Everyone must be asleep by now. Caía was sure of it; despite the fact that she normally couldn't hear anyone anyway. They were insulated upstairs, and only now and again did she ever hear their balcony doors open or close. *His mostly.* Despite Marta's room being directly above hers, Caía rarely heard footfalls overhead.

Sex was good, Caía thought again—*really, really good.*

She brought the hand with the soap to her left breast, circling her nipple, letting it rest there, feeling the thump-thump of her heart beneath her palm. And, as she lay there, she sensed a pin-prick of light at the edge of her darkness.

Why can't you want someone else? Why does it have to be him?

But she already knew the answer to that question, because it was wrapped up in the same reason she'd come to Spain.

Unable to resist temptation, Caía stood. She grabbed a towel, dried herself off, and put on her robe. She thought maybe she would stop in the bedroom, lie down on the bed and lull herself to sleep, but she didn't. She paused long enough to rough the towel through her hair, mainly so she wouldn't drip water all over the floors and give herself away, and then she hurled the wet towel onto the bed, not caring that she might return to a wet spot.

Deep down, she wasn't sure what was luring her upstairs, but she wasn't in the mood to analyze it. That she didn't pick up a candlestick on the way was promising.

She did it in the bedroom with a candlestick.

The thought brought a wry twist to her lips. Over the course of the past few weeks, Caía had found herself fantasizing about the house as a game of Clue. *She did it with poison in the kitchen. Or, it happened in the office with a gun.* Except she didn't own a gun, and she was beginning to suspect that revenge wasn't at all what had brought her to this moment. Although she wasn't sure why she was risking discovery, creeping up to the second floor, that's exactly what she did.

The house was dark, but Caía's eyes easily adjusted. Tonight, the balcony doors were all shut. Laura's bedroom door was closed. So was her mom's—both at the opposite end of the hall from Nick's. She looked toward the kitchen, telling herself that a glass of water was her objective. Certainly, that's what she would tell Marta, if Marta should happen to see her now. Or Eugenia, but Eugenia rarely ventured downstairs.

She could hear the tinkle of water in the pool below.

There was only one reason to go right . . . one bedroom in that direction—that and the salon, where she and Marta had spent so much time chatting. But this was the first time Caía had ever dared come upstairs alone at night, because she was afraid that if she did she would march into his room and strangle him where he lay.

How many times had she imagined her fingers closing around the small bones of his neck? How difficult was it to strangle a man, anyway? It looked so easy in the movies. You just wrapped your hand around his neck and squeezed. Or she could use the pillow.

Caía's bare feet left the cold marble stairs, padding quietly over old wood. It was a long, endless hall, and despite its tendency to echo, she managed to be silent.

She didn't go straight into the living room. She turned left into Nick's suite, slid past the outer foyer of his bedroom, where his closets were, and stopped, leaning against his door frame, peering into his room, surprised to find that he slept with his balcony doors open—the one that looked out onto the street.

Really, if she wanted to hurt him now, escape would be easy. There were no bars on his window, as there were on the windows downstairs. A soft, cool breeze filtered in, cooling Caía's damp skin. The scent of oranges wafted in . . . low-lying fruit.

Why are you here, Caía?

The answer lay so very still in the center of the bed, and the sight of him made Caía's heart pump a little faster. Confused, unsure of herself, she turned to leave.

"Caía?"

The sound of his voice stopped her. Her hand lifted to her throat, and the robe fell open, her nipples tightening with the breeze.

Caía didn't know what to say. What did you say when caught creeping into someone else's room in the middle of the night? Not, "Oops, I'm sorry, I took a wrong turn." She didn't belong on this floor at all. She didn't belong in this house . . . and yet, here she was . . .

"Caía," he said again, and Caía turned to face him without bothering to pinch together her robe, leaving herself exposed. She wanted him to see her, wanted him to know . . .

She could feel her body coming to life again, and she moved closer, against her better judgment. Her breath came in soft pants now, and she tried to find the will to leave.

"I've been thinking about you," he said. "Hoping you would come."

Goosebumps erupted over Caía's skin as she slid out of her robe, dropping it to the floor. She moved purposely toward the bed. Nick took her by the hand when she came within reach and pulled her the rest of the way in.

Thirteen

To protest against the universe of grief...
create happiness.
– *Albert Camus*

RIGHT. WRONG.

These were concepts that Caía understood on a basic level. Where she lived now dangerously skirted the other side of the fence.

It wasn't as though sex changed everything, but it should. *Shouldn't it?*

There had been nothing tender about their coming together. Sex was desperate and even furious, and if Nick understood what they had done—or rather, what they were doing—he never let on. They were like teenagers, sneaking around at night, trading bedrooms. If only on Caía's stronger nights he would stay in his room, it wouldn't have continued.

By day, neither of them confessed anything to Marta, but Marta wasn't stupid. You could smell pheromones in the air—or at least that's what Caía suspected.

She smelled sex all day long. What was worse, her body responded to Nick's voice. The minute he entered a room, her nipples grew hard.

Last night, after they were done, he'd kissed her gently on the forehead as Caía pretended to sleep, and then he'd crept out of her room and into the dark house. Long before he'd reached the marble stairs, there was a lingering emptiness where only seconds before there had been something else . . . something Caía would never have dreamt.

Only when she was sure he was gone, she'd lifted herself from the bed, and hid behind the palm outside her room, peering up at his balcony doors.

Did Marta know? Was she awake to see his bathroom lights flip on?

His balcony doors opened, and Caía sensed him standing there, gazing down at her room—at her—but then he went away and imagined him slipping into his bed, sated and spent. After a while, Caía moved back to her own bed, pulling the covers over her head.

Had she betrayed herself? Jack? Certainly not Gregg, because Gregg no longer had any stake in her life. Maybe she was meant to be with Nick? Not for the long-term, only for the moment. Maybe this was how they were both meant to heal?

The next morning, Caía slept late. She grabbed her iPad the instant she woke up and lay in bed, clicking through photos of Jack, taking time with each and every one, trying to envision the moments before and after each photograph was taken.

It was so strange to consider how much time she'd spent uploading her library, especially after the swiftness with which she'd dumped her household belongings into storage. *Hours and hours longer by comparison.* Whatever Gregg hadn't seen fit to take, Caía had packed up and called movers to cart over to storage. At the moment, she didn't even know where the key to the storage unit was. Maybe in one of the pockets of her suitcase. But this photo library she had accumulated was at least a hundred thousand strong—easily. Especially given the plethora of similar poses Caía could no longer find in her heart to delete. There were nearly one hundred shots in one set alone, where Jack's face—every possible expression and angle—had been captured on digital film, way more special to her now than the natural wonder they'd gone to see.

"Wow!" Jack had said, as he'd peered out over the Grand Canyon. He spread his arms, and stood on tiptoes, like an eagle in flight.

"Be careful, Jack."

"Let him be, Caía."

She was a "hover parent," Gregg sometimes said, never giving Jack any room to breathe. Caía didn't see it that way. She was sure what he meant to say was that she was a "hover wife," never giving Gregg space to carry on like he wanted to.

"Hard to imagine anyone might want to jump that, eh, Jack?"

Jack's brows crashed over his father's question. He looked at his dad. Caía captured it on film. *Click. Click. Click.*

"Evel Knievel," Gregg said.

Click. Click. Click.

"Nope," Caía argued. "It was his son, Robbie. His father never did it." She was right, of course, but Caía cared more about proving Gregg wrong than she did about enlightening their son.

For Gregg, however, the father must always be the hero of every story, and Caía saw it the other way around. *Click. Click. Click.* Their son would be a far better man than Gregg could ever think to be. Already, he had a stronger grasp of right and wrong, and knew not to lie—something Gregg had little compunction over.

Click. Click. Click.

"Yeah, whatever," her husband had said. "The point is that someone jumped it, right?" And then he'd slid Caía a look of contempt and Caía put the camera down. Deep down, she'd experienced a touch of satisfaction over having turned his story upside down.

Now, she touched the screen with a fingertip, tracing the lines of her son's jaw.

He was twelve in this photograph. Or maybe eleven. It was taken after Gregg's thirty-second birthday because he was wearing that red jacket Caía had given him the year before—the North Face windbreaker he'd been eyeing for months. Why had she bothered?

Because she was still pretending things could be different. Because instead of figuring it all out, she'd put her son second and her anger first . . . anger she'd begun nursing since long before Jack's death.

That same ugly memory fluttered at the edges of her consciousness, threatening to turn her mood dark again.

There was a soft knock at her door, and Caía put the iPad down, turning it over to hide the screen. "Yes?"

Nick opened the door. He came in, a warm smile playing upon his lips, as though he now regarded her fondly. It made her feel . . . guilty.

"Marta said she invited you to join us?"

Caía furrowed her brow.

"Zahara," he said, reminding her.

"Oh." *It was that weekend.* Caía glanced at the iPad lying on the bed, the image on the screen facing the bedspread still imprinted in her head.

"Will you come?"

Unexpectedly, hot tears sprang to Caía's eyes. Confusion wove itself through her cells, like a beginning cancer.

"Caía?" With a look of concern on his face, Nick came into the room and sat on the edge of the bed. Caía grabbed her iPad, pulling it out of his reach—a gesture that didn't go unnoticed by him, although he said nothing. Instead, he reached over to grab Caía's ankle, as though he'd sensed somehow that she was falling, and he meant to save her. "Are you sure you're not having regrets?"

"No." The word escaped before Caía could consider it. But it was the truth, she realized at once. These last few weeks she'd felt more alive than she had in years. No, she didn't regret anything at all—a fact that had her stomach tied in knots.

"Did Marta tell you why we're going?"

Caía shook her head, tears swimming in her eyes.

"You know," he said, "at times like this, I really have to believe in something bigger than us. I don't know what brought us together, Caía, but it feels . . ." He searched for a word. "Divine."

No, Caía thought frantically. There was nothing divine in their meeting. She'd followed him here, with less than noble intentions, but how could she tell him that now?

"We've all lost someone . . . your son, my brother, Laura's father . . . we're taking Jimmy's ashes somewhere he would have approved of. We—I," he amended, "want you to come."

Caía couldn't say no, even though she tried. The word simply wouldn't emerge from her lips, no matter how hard she pushed for it. "Okay," she said.

☙

"*¡Belén, campanas de Belén!*
"*Que los ángeles tocan*
"*¿Qué nueva me traéis?*"

Seated in the back seat along with her mother, Laura sang unabashedly. Off tune, she nevertheless belted out her catchy little Christmas song, all the while fanning herself with the Spanish abanico Caía had gifted her.

"Do you like my song, Tiíta?"

It took Caía a woozy moment to realize what Laura had said, and then recall that there were only two women in the car, one of which was her mother, not her aunt. Caía turned around to be sure she'd heard correctly. Laura was looking at her, smiling coyly behind her black, rose-painted fan.

Her mother caught the gesture as well, and seeing Caía's startled expression, gently chided her child. "Caía is not your tía, Laura."

"But, yes, I want her to be my tiíta," the child said. "Because . . ." She pushed her palm into the air. "I really don't have one."

Despite her momentary horror, Caía bit her lip to keep from laughing at that perfectly reasonable explanation. Nick slid Caía a glance, one that said too little and too much during the brief instant before his gaze returned to the road—a split second later.

I swear to God, he'd said.

Just a split second.

Just a split second.

Morbidly, Caía envisioned the car jetting off the road, pummeling down into a gorge, never to be seen or heard from again. But of course, she didn't want that fate for Laura, nor for Marta, nor for Nick.

Vast olive groves dominated the horizon. Closer to the narrow mountain road there were succulents, cacti and rosemary. It was a curiously Southwestern vista, arid and patchy, in thirsty shades of green and brown. She watched Nick driving, analyzing the casual, confident way he held the wheel, not unlike the driver's stance her husband had so often taken—as though he'd been born behind the wheel and the car was merely an extension of himself.

Jack would never get that opportunity. This was not something Caía was ever bound to know about her son—whether he would grow into the same confident demeanor.

In the driver's seat, Nick's eyes rarely left the road—a good thing, because the landscape turned jagged as they wended their way into the sierras.

"Caía, don't you like to be my tiíta?" Laura persisted, her voice pouty.

Once again, Caía glanced uncomfortably at Nick. There was something surreal about the moment—as though none of it couldn't possibly be happening . . . as though it must be a twisted dream she was having. God, maybe she was still locked away in that hospital, waiting endlessly for Gregg to arrive?

"Caía?"

"Laura," her mother chastened. "¿Que pesada!"

"It's okay," Caía said. "We can pretend . . . for today."

"No," Laura said, kicking her feet against Nick's seat. "Not for today," she argued. "Tomorrow and every, every day, *vale*?"

Her mother laughed, probably embarrassed. Nick chuckled too, despite Laura's pummeling of his seat. But, here again, he didn't take his eyes off the road.

It was difficult not to be amused or charmed by Laura's impetuosity, especially when the sentiment was so sweet. But she was getting tired. "Laura," her mother said once again, and Nick reached over to squeeze Caía's hand, a silent thank you. The gesture made Caía's heart beat faster. She slid her hand out from under his palm, uncomfortable with the show of affection. Thinking about her father, Caía peered out the window, letting herself be hypnotized by the olive groves, and with every olive tree they passed came a new missed opportunity to say what should have been said—to extend an olive branch.

I'm sorry, Jack.
I'm sorry, Laura.
I'm sorry, Nick.
I'm sorry, Marta.
I'm sorry, Daddy.
I'm sorry, Gregg.

Fourteen

*The darker the night,
the brighter the stars . . .*
– *Fyodor Dostoyevsky*

CHICAGO, WEDNESDAY, JUNE 15, 2016, 10:00 A.M.
CAÍA

"HEY, MA?"
Caía stared at the computer screen. She heard Jack calling, but couldn't shake off her stupor.
"Ma?"
He sounded irritated. Finally, Caía looked up at him, blinking as she met her son's resentful blue eyes. He looked so much like his dad, it made her heart hurt. It was difficult to look at him now and not see Gregg, and sometimes, lately, she didn't look very hard at all.
It didn't help much that he was developing Gregg's attitude. At thirteen, Jack was already a head taller than Gregg, but lanky, as though he hadn't been fed properly in weeks. To the contrary, he ate like a horse, shoving more carbs down his throat in a single day than Caía could eat in a year. Bag of chips. *Gone.* Yesterday's leftover mac 'n' cheese. *Gone.* Pizza. *Gone.* Now, he stood in the doorway with a soda in his hand, and Caía didn't have the energy to ask him where it came from, because she knew. *His dad.* Gregg subverted her authority every chance he got, minimizing Caía in any way

possible. It was as though he had to prove a point—that he was the man of this house, and as such, he was the one in charge.

She hated that most about him, especially where it concerned their son. All the things she'd once loved—that charming Georgia drawl, his unflagging machismo—she hated now. She centered her gaze on the can. "Did your father buy you that?"

Jack peered down at his soda, brushing his bangs aside nonchalantly, like the star member of a boy band. "Yeah," he said, and took a sip as Caía watched, tossing it down like his dad might have done. As though it were a challenge.

Where did her sweet little boy go?

Where are you, Jack?

"You know I don't like you drinking those, Jack."

She'd said his name that way again, like she so often did his dad's. He flinched. "It's just one, Mom! Jesus!"

Caía's patience was thin. "Don't use God's name in vain, Jack."

"Why not? It's not like you care. We don't believe in God."

We, he said, as though there were a consensus. *We don't believe in God.* But there wasn't any *we* here in this house. "Your father doesn't believe in God. I don't believe in religion. There's a difference, Jack."

"Whatever," Jack said, and Caía bristled.

No other word ever grated on her nerves the way that one did. *Whatever.* Gregg said it so often these days, and now it was bleeding into her son's vocabulary. She slid a furious glance toward the computer screen. If her eyes could shoot missiles, the computer would have been pulverized on the spot. "What do you want, Jack?"

"Can I go to the park?"

"Is your room clean?"

"Yeah," he said, and as though to make a point, he took his brand-new smartphone out of his pocket—the one Caía said he couldn't have. Of course, his father gave it to him, despite Jack taking his last phone apart. It was not a birthday present. Gregg claimed he had a new work phone, but Caía suspected he was paying for a separate plan, just so she couldn't check his phone records. She stared at her son, hating that she didn't believe him. His father was proving to be a proficient liar. Maybe it was in the genes?

"Go check if you want. I just wanna go now. Can I, please?"

Taking in a breath, Caía peered down at her computer—at the open email on the screen, sent to her by mistake. Or maybe it wasn't by mistake at all. There was the difference of a single letter: *c.paine@webmail.com* rather than *g.paine*. But on a keyboard, it would have to have been a purposeful mistake. "I'm free," it read. "No sessions this afternoon. Meet you at noon. Village Tap. Kisses for all your nasty bits. Love, L."

The Village Tap was here in their neighborhood, just a stone's throw from their house. That he—and she—would add insult to injury by meeting right under her nose, where neighbors went to grab a beer after work . . . it really pissed Caía off.

He'd promised her it was over, and Caía stayed because she didn't want Jack to end up a child of divorce. But the truth was that none of them were happy, and Jack was the one who was changing most because of it. *Leave, take him with you, right now*, a little voice urged. *Before it's too late.*

"Ma?"

Caía peered up at her son, noting the angry set of his pale blue eyes. She made a sound fraught with frustration. "Yeah, go."

He turned so swiftly, Caía didn't have a chance to add another word. She heard the front door open and slam, and she returned to staring at her screen, feeling old and tired. And rejected. And ugly. And judged. But, of course. But why should it come down to not feeling good enough? As though Gregg were any sort of prize.

"Hey, it's over," he'd said. "It's all over, okay?" And then he'd taken Caía into his arms and pushed her head against his shoulder, patting the back of her head, as though she were his pet. "There's nothing going on, Caía," he'd said, contradicting himself. "Nothing happened. Do you believe me?"

All her evidence was sketchy. She had to give him that. Even this email was sketchy. For all Caía knew, Lindsey was messing with her head. There was no doubt in her mind that the email was inappropriately personal. No doubt it was from her. It was sent from her email address. But if she'd sent it to Caía on purpose, then she must want Caía to know they were still seeing each other, despite Gregg's assurances to the contrary.

What was more, she wanted Caía to catch them.

Apparently, Gregg was a liar, and neither Caía nor Lindsey had the wherewithal to let him go. But Lindsey was wrong about that, because Caía only needed to know the truth, and then she could leave with a clear conscience.

She could stay with her pop, take Jack. Her father would welcome them. He was lost without her mother, and he and Jack were still very close. But until Caía actually saw Gregg and Lindsey together with her own two eyes, she needed to try to believe her husband . . . for Jack's sake.

It was an easy enough thing to prove, right? If she walked down to the Village Tap and both Lindsey and Gregg were there, it was over. If she went and found only Lindsey, it was entirely possible this was a last-ditch effort from a conniving witch.

And if neither of them were there... then what? Did she simply close her computer and walk away, never say another word about it, and keep trying?

Caía glanced at the time stamp on her screen: It was 11:17 a.m. If she hurried, she could be home long before Jack returned from the park. She jumped up from the couch, leaving the computer open, but then, thinking of Jack, she went back and slowly closed the screen.

☙

ZAHARA DE LA SIERRA, SPAIN, PRESENT DAY

Perched high in the Andalusian hills, the white village of Zahara was less than an hour and a half's drive from Jeréz. Originally occupied by the Moors, the eagle's nest settlement overlooked a valley with a sprawling blue lake. Remnants of its Moorish history were everywhere, but none more prominent than the fortress on the hill. It was there they were headed, to the top—a steep, rocky climb that made Caía question the state of her health.

Along the narrow, cobbled path, cacti lined the way instead of rails. Certainly, this was no place that should be sanctioned for little children. There should have been a sign at the beginning of the trail that read: "Kids yay high, no way." For that matter, adults had no business here, either—at least not without proper gear, which of course Caía didn't have. Even her Doc Martens would have been questionable here, although sandals were downright treacherous. She felt as though she were scaling a cliff in slippery skis. Every now and again, she hit a patch of slick rock, and slid backward, teetering a bit like she did on ice skates. In fact, it was like climbing one of those gym obstacles, like the one at their gym, where Gregg and Caía used to compete, only this one went on forever and wasn't precisely as steep.

"Nice going," Lindsey had said, cheering Gregg on. *Clap. Clap. Clap.* After a while, Gregg stopped asking Caía to join him, claiming that she held him back.

She'd held him back, all right.

Breathless and far from sure-footed, Caía nevertheless kept pace, determined not to allow a five-year-old outdo her. Not to mention her uncle, who seemed wholly unfazed by the steep, narrow climb. It was a sad, sad day when Caía allowed herself to measure her actions by that of a child's. But there it was.

On the way up Nick offered a history lesson, his voice steady and sure, with no sign that his lecture would ever put him out of breath.

On the other hand, Caía was forced to stop every so often, pretending to take in the magnificent view as she gulped in a breath.

Simply for effect, she snapped photos with her cell phone, intending to delete them all later. She didn't need mementos of today—not when she was bound to leave. And even if she didn't firebomb everything and tell Nick the truth, there was no way this could have a happy-ever-after. Lies were no way to begin a relationship—particularly not lies of this magnitude.

"Hey, Nick? You killed my son, and guess what, I followed you here—why? Because I fantasized about killing you."

No, it was a pending disaster—even more so than this climb up the hill. In fact, it might end better if she dropped dead of a heart attack on the way up, or if Nick fell and broke his neck. That's how dire the situation was, and there didn't appear to be an easy way out.

"Back when the Moors held Zahara," Nick regaled his niece, "the city was occupied only by men."

Her sweet five-year-old voice brimmed with curiosity. "Where was they mamas, Tiíto?"

"At home," he said, as though he knew.

"But whyyy? Why was they at home, Tiíto Nick?"

"Because, only men were allowed to come here," he explained, with more patience than Caía had at the moment. She wanted to give up, go back down . . . go home . . . pack her bags . . . "See that castle up there?"

"Uh-huh."

"It was built during the thirteenth century—more than eight hundred years ago. That's a looonng time. They call it la Torre del Homenaje, because that's where people used to pay homage to the lords of the house of Ponce de León."

"I don't know those people, Tiíto. Y no sé qué es un *omage.*"

"Well . . ." He thought about it. "That's where knights— you know what a knight is, right?" She nodded. "It's where they pledged loyalty to their king—el rey—and promised to obey his laws."

"Like when I tell Mami I will be good?"

"Something like that."

"Mi papá me dijo que mami es la reina de mi casa."

Her mother was the queen of their house. It must have been nice to be so revered. Caia thought about Gregg, and tried to recall how it was in the beginning. She'd been so enamored with him, and really, she'd been so grateful for his attentions that she'd promised him the world. A rush of sadness overcame her—sorrow for the youngsters they had been. Regret was such an ugly sentiment. There was so much Caía would do differently if she had it to do all over again, but maybe it was time to forgive herself—and Gregg—and move on.

Caía stopped again, taking in the view, overdosing on the bittersweet familiarity of the conversation. She inhaled a breath, exhaling slowly. Olive trees grew everywhere, but here more than in Jeréz, it was the scent of orange blossoms that filled the air, even in the middle of November.

Along the edges of the path grew wild cucumbers. Caía had never seen any quite so tiny, and never in the wild. They would be ideal for pickling. She meant to stop and pick one to give it a closer inspection, but she had already lingered too long and, not wanting to be left behind, she hurried to catch up, leaving the cucumbers for later. Pinching her jacket together to stay warm, she moved behind Nick, because the higher they climbed, the windier it got, and he made a great windshield. Right now, even her toes were cold, and what was worse, if she wasn't slipping and sliding, she was stubbing her toes on the rocks.

Around the midway point, between the overlook and the tower, they passed what appeared to be a mass of old ruins. Probably having noticed her struggling, Nick came over and took Caía by the hand. "Bedouin huts," he said, pointing to the ruins and guiding her up the path. Marta spied his gesture and smiled, taking her daughter by the hand and hurrying up ahead to give them privacy.

Caía tried to free her hand, but Nick held it firmly. "It's steep here," he said.

"I'm a big girl," Caía reassured him, and shook her hand free, half embarrassed, and maybe half annoyed at herself for the mess she'd created.

Up ahead, Laura crawled like a spider on four legs. Marta lifted her up, carrying her. Feeling like an intruder in a special moment, Caía stopped again, her emotions getting the better of her. From the top of the hill, they intended to launch Jimmy's ashes on Chinese lanterns. They'd brought along a picnic snack, which Nick carried in his backpack. But she shouldn't be here. What was she doing holding his hand?

Admittedly, the view from this height was spectacular, especially with the sun shining over the bright blue lake. One glimpse of the turquoise-blue waters of the Embalse de Zahara and it was difficult to imagine why Ponce de León would ever go searching elsewhere for the Fountain of Youth. She peered up the hill, at Marta and her child. Both disappeared around the bend.

"Even big girls need help now and again," Nick said. "Big boys do too." He put one arm around Caía's waist and drew her close, kissing her nose.

Hating herself for it, Caía gave into the desire to be held. "So, you're saying you need me to hold your hand?"

He smiled. "Maybe."

For a blissful moment, Caía stood there, looking at Nick—his winsome smile and little boy eyes—and realized that she could never have hurt him. Even now, in the broad light of day, with Marta and Laura traipsing up ahead, she wanted to take her hands out of her pockets and put her arms around his waist and hold him tight. Loss was a touchstone for depression, she realized. Depression was a sort of madness. She was well acquainted with that form of insanity, but in her darkest hour, when it seemed no relief would be forthcoming, it showed up in the most unexpected place . . . in the arms of the man she'd thought she wanted to kill.

What a pair they were.

Where to go from here.
Only one way.
Down.

Nick turned his back to her, looking over the horizon. They were up so high now that an eagle flew by, but the castle was higher yet.

Nick had his back to Caía, giving her time to rest. He stepped close to the edge, peering below, as though daring her to push him off.

She moved closer . . . so close she might have put her hand on the small of his back . . . but she didn't. She didn't even take her hands out of her pockets. Some part of her longed to comfort Nick, but she didn't dare. Her emotions were even closer to the edge than he was. "It's so beautiful," she said.

"Gorgeous." He turned to look at her over his shoulder. "Jimmy proposed to Marta up there," he said, pointing to the castle on the summit. The narrow path wound itself about the hill. Marta and Laura were on the other side of the mountain now, and if they stayed in this spot long enough, they might reappear on a shelf above.

Succulents, cacti, and rosemary thrived, but barely anything else. It was more like a promontory, craggy and rocky, with paths that wandered dangerously close to the edge—like the spot where Nick was standing now. But despite its desolate appearance, the land it governed was gorgeous. Serene. Never ending. Olive groves for miles.

It made sense that Marta would wish to come here to let Jimmy go.

It was time to do that for Jack as well.

Caía peered up at the castle, pulling her jacket tighter, wishing things could have been different. And once again, her gaze fell on more of those little wild cucumbers near Nick's feet. She took one hand out of her pocket, reaching to pick one to inspect it, hoping to move on to another subject. "What are these?"

"Exploding cucumbers," he said, just as Caía touched one.

In the blink of an eye, she saw Nick's car driving down the road . . . her son nearing the crosswalk, perfectly aligned, a perfect storm.

Seeds burst from the cucumber pod, shooting into Caía's eyes. The impact was violent, like a BB in the eye. Caía squealed, leaping back, losing her footing. The back of her sandal caught on a rock. Through teary eyes, she saw the fear in Nick's gaze and reached for him—too late.

Nick's arm shot out, grasping at thin air as Caía plummeted backward, free-falling until she grabbed for a thorny cactus, shredding the skin on her hand.

Yowling in pain, she let go again . . . peering up into Nick's eyes. And this, she thought, before she felt the impact, was the last face her son had spied before he died.

This was not the way Caía meant for anything to end.

But this was the thing, right? Things don't necessarily end up the way you think they should. Like maybe you believe you're going to be happy all your life, and suddenly you're not. Or maybe you think revenge is what you need, and it turns out it's not. All you ever needed or wanted was to commiserate with someone who understands.

Fifteen

And we wept that one so lovely
should have a life so brief.
– *William Cullen Bryant*

CHICAGO, WEDNESDAY, JUNE 15, 2016
CAÍA

OH, GOD! JACK'S CAKE.

Caía was supposed to have picked it up by 2:00 p.m. She'd almost forgotten, and the realization came to her as she sat staring at the Village Tap's front door. The green neon sign above the glass door read: Beer Garden. The windows were clean. There was no one outside.

No Lindsey. No Gregg.

She'd been so wrapped up in Lindsay's email this morning that she didn't even remember to wish her son happy birthday. No wonder he'd had attitude. He probably thought she'd forgotten. Well, she didn't forget, but admittedly, she did forget a lot these days. Her head was so wrapped up in her failing marriage. She and Gregg walked through their house like strangers, barely looking at one another, barely tolerating each other, and her son had become a hungry ghost.

After all this was over, Caía intended to make it up to him. But right now, she needed to call him and tell him happy birthday. The problem was that she was already two beers in, and such a lightweight. And her whole life was on the verge of change.

From Caía's vantage at the back of the bar, she could see everyone who walked through the front door. *Noon*, the email had said. *Noon.* She glanced at her cell phone, checking the time. Five more minutes, and then she would go home—even if they did come in. The point was for them to see her, and for Caía to see them. But, of course, she wouldn't tell Jack. Not today. She'd leave here and go pick up his cake, and then go home, and give him his present, and then... and then...

But what if she called and slurred her words? What if he asked where she was? Caía was a terrible liar. She set the phone down again, waiting just another moment... and then she picked it up and punched in her son's number.

The waitress came over, and Caía put a hand to her throat, making the kill sign. One way or the other, she was out of here in five minutes. "Come on, Jack, answer," she said, her eyes glued to the front door. When he didn't, she checked the time again—12:02 p.m. She hung up, waited another moment, and tried one more time. This time it went straight to voicemail.

Finally, finally! Lindsey walked in, and Caía found herself reluctant to leave. She ordered one more beer, feeling in her gut that Gregg would follow any moment. She hid her face as Lindsey walked past, making her way to the back, into the beer garden. Such a cozy spot, with awnings over the patio. Vines on the brick wall. She and Gregg used to nestle in a corner.

Any minute now and it will all be over.

A sense of excitement bubbled through Caía's veins, because finally, finally she would learn the truth. She would have a reason to leave.

JACK

He loved the sound of his wheels turning over the pavement, the rumble beneath his feet. It wasn't a sound that could be imitated by anyone.

A memory popped into Jack's head—of his mom seated on the living room floor going, "Vroom, vroom, vroom." It made him smile, but only for a second, and then he remembered.

Everything was shit.

Lately, this was the only time he was happy—on his skateboard.

He wasn't stupid. He knew what was up. His parents looked at each other like they hated one another. And his mother—the one person he counted on most—she sometimes looked at him now like he was a spider crawling out from under a bed.

It was that same look she gave his dad, and it made him angry. This was the reason he sometimes took his father's side, because he knew it would piss her off.

This morning, she'd been so wrapped up in whatever stupid thing she'd found on her computer that she wouldn't even look him in the eyes, and then, when she did, it was all about, "Jack, Jack, Jack. Did you clean your room, Jack? Where'd you get the Coke, Jack?" *Jack, Jack, Jack.* In that hateful way she sometimes said his name, maybe like everything was all his fault.

Noise was all it was, just noise.

It's my birthday, man.

He wished they would get it all over with. He wished that his mother would stop pretending. Yeah, he wanted to piss her off, because that was the only time she didn't remind him of a zombie, walking around with that dead look on her face. She wouldn't like that he'd gone to Millennium Park today, and she probably thought he was going somewhere closer to home, but what did it matter? By the time she figured out he was gone, he would be home again.

Way back in the day, when things were different, she used to tell him "happy birthday" even before he ever got out of bed, and now she couldn't even remember.

What was she? Like eighty or something? What was wrong with her head? Even Pop called to wish him happy birthday on his brand-new phone.

Once again, the phone buzzed in his pocket, and Jack wondered if it could be his mom. Some part of him wanted to keep her guessing, except he knew he wouldn't do that.

Skating along, he fished the cell phone out of his pocket and stared at the number on the screen, paying no attention to the walk sign, telling him when it was okay to cross.

It was 12:02 p.m.

It was her, probably wanting him to come home already. Maybe she went and checked his room. Or maybe she was going to finally tell him happy birthday. Or maybe she just wanted to yell at him some more. Jack looked up—and screamed.

The impact knocked him off his skateboard. He heard the crack of wood beneath a tire as he flew up, over the car's silver hood. Somehow, he managed to hang tight to his new phone, but it went flying out of his hand when he hit his head. "Mom," he said.

It was the last word he ever said.

Sixteen

Forgiveness is the attribute
of the strong.
– *Mahatma Gandhi*

CHICAGO, SATURDAY, JUNE 18, 2016
CAÍA

CAÍA FELT A HAND ON HER SHOULDER, RUBBING GENTLY. She recognized her father's touch and a tear slid past her guard. He didn't speak. He rarely did, unless he had something important to say; otherwise, he had that soothing way about him that needed no words to convey his love.

Strong and silent, steadfast and loyal, her pop had been her touchstone all her life. He comforted her now as he had that day so long ago when Caía ran home crying over Robbie Bowles. Up until now, no matter what befell her, Caía always knew her dad would be there to help her pull her socks up and keep on marching.

But not this time.
No one can help me this time.

"He can't hear me," she said softly. "He can't hear me anymore, Daddy. I talk and talk and talk . . . but he can't hear me." She cried softly, brokenhearted.

Her father pulled her close, with more strength in his frail old arms than a man of ninety-seven should have. And with her daddy at her side, Caía worked up the nerve to reach out and touch the shining teakwood casket, hoping to feel her son.

It was cold and smooth, like glass...

They called her first—someone at the scene. Caía hadn't answered. Because she didn't recognize the number. They called his father next, and of course, Gregg went running. That's why he never showed up at the Village Tap. He'd called Caía as well, but Caía was so tuned into Lindsey that she hadn't dared answer a phone call from her own husband. How long did she sit there waiting for Gregg to come in? Nursing yet another beer, waiting, waiting, waiting... for what?

She had been so sure Gregg would come. So sure. And so she'd sat there, all the while planning all the terrible things she would say to him. Meantime, a few blocks south, her son's lifeless body was being hauled into an ambulance.

"You want to go with him?" her father said. He stopped petting her and let his hand rest upon her arm, trembling slightly. He was too old to travel, she thought numbly. She'd told him not to come because she fully intended on going home to Georgia after the funeral. At least for a while. Caía swallowed but didn't answer, knowing instinctively that he wouldn't like what she had to say. Gregg was across the room, still on his phone. No doubt talking to her. But at least he had the decency not to invite her here. Although even if he had, Caía wasn't so sure she would have cared. She was numb inside.

Cold.
Dead.
Like her son.

"Caía," her father said quietly. "Your place is here."

Caía flicked another glance across the room, at Gregg. *Not with him.* "There's nothing left for me, Pop," she said, lifting a hanky to her nose, secure in the knowledge that her father couldn't possibly understand how she felt. Her depth of despair was far too great. And she didn't mean just here, in

Chicago. She meant anywhere. She couldn't picture any life without her son.

She moved her hand over the cold casket, mimicking the way her father had caressed her back, and, after a long moment, Caía met her father's pale blue eyes, clouded with age.

There was evidence of cataracts forming in his eyes. Why hadn't she noticed? Naturally, he had adored Jack, his only grandchild, and nothing would have kept him from the funeral. But for the first time in Caía's life, she saw her father as less than hale. He was no longer the quiet, looming giant he had once been. For a moment, she was lost, blinking as she peered into the mirror of her father's eyes. And she realized . . . he felt exactly what she felt. He loved her, but he wanted to be with her mother. "You have no room to talk," she said, returning her gaze to the casket.

How could he ask her to stay if he didn't want to be here, himself?

"Ah, Caía. You think there is nothing left for you now, no tears left to shed, but drop by drop, there will be an ocean of your tears before you leave this world. And, one day, you will know what it means to want to stay."

Caía swallowed over the lump in her throat. "You don't know what you're talking about, Dad." Silence wedged between them. Snippets of whispered conversations came in and out of focus, forcing their way into Caía's bubble.

"There must be trouble in paradise, right?" "Look at him over there on his cell phone." "So sad." "Well, yeah, but I would never, ever let my son skate out in traffic like that."

"Caía," her dad said, dragging her back.

Caía couldn't look at him. She didn't want to look at anyone. There was a tsunami building deep down, and if she let go, she would weep, and she wouldn't stop weeping until everyone in this room lay six-feet underwater.

"Caía," he said again, very soberly, "I never thought to burden you with this . . . but I see now that it has a purpose. When your mother and I left Poland . . . we left a boy . . ."

For a moment, she wasn't sure she'd heard him right, and then her gaze snapped to meet her father's, her eyes wide with horror over the implication of his confession. "What do you mean you left a boy?"

His eyes glistened with unshed tears. "A son," he said, and clenched his trembling jaw, but he did not avert his gaze. It was a stoic, sad look Caía had glimpsed a hundred thousand times on her father, but never once had she wondered if he could be mourning a child. He pursed his lips, but they defied him, trembling.

Caía blinked. "Pop . . . are you telling me I had a brother?"

He nodded—a gesture that looked more like a man choking. And then he cleared his throat. "Your mama and I . . . we wished to stay. But your baba said go." He was faraway now, as he told her this, and Caía shuddered. "She said she would send Stefan when it was safe."

Stefan. Goosebumps erupted on Caía's arms and legs.

Sorrow, like stone weights, sank into the depths of her heart. Just when it seemed her grief couldn't reach greater depths . . . there was this . . .

"They never made it?"

It wasn't a question. She knew the answer. There had been no pictures of that boy, Stefan, no pictures anywhere, but how could there have been? He was a child conceived in a time of war by a young couple who could have been no more than children themselves. Her father and mother had always been such sober people, doting on Caía throughout her life. But then, of course, they would have wished to protect their only surviving child—even from the truth.

All that had ever mattered to either of them was to provide Caía with a good home. All their quiet evenings, their stoic silences, and heartfelt looks . . . the picture of her baba on the dresser, the only one that existed in their home. All of it made horrifying sense.

"They never made it," her father said, and his entire face seemed to quiver with emotion. His paper-thin flesh turned translucent pink. "But we had each other, Caía. And we had you."

She understood what he was trying to say, and there were things Caía probably should have said, but she couldn't think of any of them. She couldn't think of anything at all. *What was he like? This boy, Stefan? Did he have the same blue eyes?*

Her father slipped into his native tongue. "Komu pora, temu czas." *When it's time, you have to go.* "But not yet," he said. "An old man, on the other hand, has no reason to stay." He too flicked a glance across the room, toward Gregg, who was holed up in a corner with his cell phone.

"Bądź odważny," her father said, patting her gently. "Be brave." And then he hugged her tight for a long time before walking away, red-faced and physically depleted by their conversation. Caía let him go, for now, so he might find himself a corner to sit and recover. There was so much to say. So much to be said. But not here, not now.

The next day, her dad insisted upon keeping his return flight to Athens. Caía assured him she would see him soon as she drove him to the airport, unable to cry, even when she saw him to the gate. She'd been so sure nothing more could happen. But she had been so wrong.

And her father was gone barely a month later, leaving Caía with more questions than answers.

You'd think a bombshell like that might be dropped over coffee—that it should come with closure. You didn't expect to find out you had a brother, and then suddenly the one person who could answer any of your questions would be . . . *poof, gone.*

Anger was easier to process.

How could her father leave her with this knowledge? How could he leave her without helping her tie up everything in a neat little bow? How could he leave her here with no one? *Alone!*

ತಿ

SPAIN, PRESENT DAY

There were moments in life that were excruciatingly ironic. This was one of them, Caía realized, as she peered up into Nick Kelly's face. What were the chances both she and her son would lock gazes with the same man during the final moments of their lives?

Except that Caía was alive, judging by the ache in her ribs . . . and her arm . . . and her head . . . and her heart. She had a concussion, two broken ribs, a fractured knee that would take some physical therapy, plus a dislocated wrist and deep scrapes from having grabbed a gnarly cactus on the way down. Fortunately, the cactus broke her fall just enough so that when she came down on her knee on the shelf below, it didn't suffer the full impact of her weight after a six-foot drop. Nevertheless, Caía felt the impact and blacked out. She rolled down another eight feet, smacking her head against the foundation of one of the Bedouin huts.

"Welcome back," Nick said.

At least a day's worth of whiskers shadowed his well-defined jaw. His dark green eyes were closer to black, his pupils overlarge. Leaving Marta and Laura, Nick had rushed down the hillside to the overlook, and there, he called for help. Caía only vaguely recalled the ride to the hospital in the back of his car. They didn't wait for an ambulance, because Caía had apparently lifted her head on her own, glassy eyed, freaking about her iPad. "Don't touch it!" she'd screamed. "Where's my iPad?"

Perhaps she'd thought she'd brought it with her, and maybe she'd broken it during her fall. But, really, Caía couldn't recall what she was thinking. Aside from the fact that her iPad contained access to her photos, she wasn't particularly attached to the device itself. She had considered the eventuality of its loss, and had uploaded all her photos to the cloud, leaving only a select few on the device and her favorite set as the sleep-mode background.

Looking her straight in the eyes, Nick laid the iPad down on the bed, beside her. Caía didn't reach for it. She couldn't. She didn't try. She didn't know what to say. *Thank you?*

"He has your eyes," he said.

The muscles in Caía's throat tightened. Words refused to form.

There was no condemnation in his gaze, only sadness. "I turned it on to see if we could . . . get numbers . . . to contact your . . ."

"Next of kin?"

He gave her a half-hearted smile. "No. The doctor needed permission to treat you, and we didn't know who to call."

Caía turned away. "And what?"

"What, what?"

"Did you reach . . . someone?"

"Yes," he said softly, and Caía turned again to face him, tears swimming in her eyes. *Who*, she wanted to ask, but pride wouldn't allow it. *Who was left? No one.*

His dark eyes were like mirrors, reflecting Caía's grief. "I recognized him right away," he managed to say, over the lump visible in his throat.

"Jack," she said, testing the name. "His name is Jack . . . my son . . ."

He nodded soberly. "I had a feeling I knew you, Caía."

"I'm sorry," she said, and meant it. She pushed her head back into the pillow, in terrible pain—not just her body, but her heart and soul.

"I get it," he said.

࿐

Life was messy, Nick thought, as he studied the woman lying in the hospital bed. She was broken in ways he feared doctors might never fix.

Deep in his gut, he must have realized who she was. The kinship they'd shared had been far deeper than anything he should have for a woman simply because they were both from the same hometown. She stubbornly avoided his gaze, staring at the door, as though hoping it would open and someone might burst through and prevent their discussion.

"Were you ever going to tell me, Caía?"

She made a slight movement he thought might have been a shrug. "I don't know," she confessed, and when she turned to look at him again, there were tears glistening in her eyes. "How long have you known?"

"The instant I turned on your iPad," he said. "If I live a million years, I will never forget his face."

Caía began to sob then, in earnest, turning her face so far to one side that it seemed she would break her neck. Nick reached out, gently touching her left arm, uncertain which parts of her didn't hurt. If he hadn't been around to see it happen, he wouldn't have known this was the same woman. Her face was swollen, her skin black and blue. There was edematous swelling beneath the skin of her face, and an orbital floor fracture in her left eye. Her hair had been shaved on one side to stitch up a wound. The blood loss frightened him. Only later was he reassured that head wounds sometimes seemed worse than they were, because the scalp was riddled with blood vessels. Fortunately, they were right; it looked worse than it was. Caía's ribs would heal quickly. Her wrist as well. The knee would take time and therapy. Nick petted her arm, waiting quietly for her sobs to subside. Finally, she swallowed and asked, "Does Marta know?"

"Yes."

"Does she hate me?"

"No."

She swallowed again. "Laura?"

"She doesn't know, Caía."

And then she turned her face again, tears streaming down her cheeks and went back to staring at the door, with trembling lips.

Nick wasn't about to allow her to ignore him. Wherever they went from here, it was better to leave nothing unsaid. "I need to know, Caía . . . what did you expect to do?"

Caía shook her head. She pursed her lips, refusing more sobs. She looked like she was on the verge of having a fit, her face red, and her body shuddering violently. "I don't know," she said. "I don't know." And then she met his gaze, and in her eyes Nick saw what he needed to see. She cried, and he let her, and then she said, "Mostly, I guess I needed to know he wasn't forgotten."

Nick nodded, thinking back to that sunny Wednesday in June—a day not even a lobotomy would help him forget. Deep down in his soul, even if he didn't actively think of it, it was a horror he would relive until the day he died. It defined him now, his every decision, his every waking move. "I remember," he said. "I will always remember, Caía."

She blinked a few tears from the corners of her eyes, then wiped them away. "He was a good boy . . . Jack was . . . he was . . . my whole life." More tears, silent and heartrending. And then, after a while, she said, brokenheartedly, "It was his birthday, did you know?"

Nick felt a stab at his chest, but it was a familiar pang he lived with every day, some days more intensely than others. He shook his head. Tears pricked at his own eyes.

Not once during their time together had she ever asked him to elaborate on the actual event—all the gory details. If she were to ask him now, he would tell her, but there was nothing significant he could add that would make her feel better. He wasn't speeding that day. He didn't run any lights. He wasn't on his phone, despite the fact that he did turn to look at it for that split second. Jack Lawrence Paine—a good-looking kid from Roscoe Village, with dirty-blond hair like his mom's, and expressive blue eyes—had skated directly into his path.

Nick remembered odd bits from that fateful moment—the metallic glint of a cell phone in Jack's hand, the wide, terrified eyes, and, most of all, he remembered the final parting of his lips—a single-syllabic formation of his mouth that might have been a moan of pain, but Nick thought he'd called for his mom. For one terrifying moment after his car came to a complete stop, he'd stared at the half of Jack's face that lay so still on his windshield, blood trickling from one corner of his mouth. For one split second, he saw the life in that boy's eyes, and then, the very next instant, as though someone flipped a switch, it was extinguished. By the time Nick stumbled out of his car, dazed and scared half out of his mind, there was a gathering crowd.

"Oh, my God," one woman said. "Oh, my God! Is he dead?"

"Doctor!" someone screamed. "We need a doctor!"

Someone else took hold of Nick's arm, maybe because his legs didn't seem to want to support him. "I saw the whole thing," some lady said. "He skated right smack in front of your car. Just like that. My dear, you couldn't have stopped. Nobody could have stopped. Don't worry, I'll stay and talk to the police. What a shame. What a shame."

All these years, Nick had held himself responsible, despite realizing on a logical level it could truly have happened to anyone. It made sense to him that the boy's mom would blame him as well . . . except he didn't see any condemnation in Caía's eyes, not anymore. What he saw now was a look of defeat . . . a woman in pain. He slid his hand down her bruised and battered arm, and nestled it in the palm of her hand. She closed her fingers around his, attempting to squeeze.

"Where do we go from here?"

It was a fine question. Nick thought about it a moment. Where could they possibly go from here? "We forgive ourselves, forgive each other, maybe start again . . . as friends?"

"I'd like that," Caía said, and they sat together in the hush that followed, she in her hospital bed, and Nick in the chair beside her, silently holding her hand.

A Life so Fair

WITH MORE THAN THREE MILLION WHEELCHAIRS IN USE IN THE U.S. ALONE, IT WAS SAFE TO SAY NO, LIFE ISN'T ALL THAT FAIR. If Caía had a mind to, she could list pages and pages of things that weren't, and could never be described as fair. *The Holocaust. Poverty. Hunger. Abuse.* Pick up a newspaper—any newspaper—on any given day; add twenty new items to your list.

It was a hard pill to swallow for a naïve girl from Athens, Georgia, whose parents had loved her so completely that life could seem to be nothing less than fair.

But Caía saw her parents in a whole new light now—the points of light in their eyes that, like Marta's, had been both happy and sad. Those emotions must seem complete dichotomies, but in truth, they were like facets of a diamond that didn't diminish its sparkle. Rather, they intensified it.

Their sadness for the child they'd lost never lessened the love they'd felt for Caía. And Caía realized now that their love for her had never diminished the grief they'd felt for Stefan. Her parents had devoted their lives to making sure Caía never doubted their love for her—as Marta had done for Laura. Caía had basked in her share of love, and Stefan's share as well. But this was the thing about love—and it wasn't a platitude—the more you gave, the more you had to give.

Love, like anger, or fear, was a choice to be made.

That day, on that hill, Caía might have made any number of choices and there might have been a different outcome.

If only she'd accepted Nick's proffered hand, perhaps they might have strolled uneventfully to the top of the hill and shared a poignant moment with a little girl and her grieving mom.

Together, they might have scattered Jimmy's ashes, lifted to the winds in Chinese lanterns. Caía could actually envision this in her head... a trio of white lanterns launched at sunset, after a picnic on the summit. *So dramatic.* There would be tears, of course, but there would have been laughter as well, because it was difficult to wallow in sorrow with a precocious five-year-old running around. "¡Mira! ¡Mira!" Laura would have shouted, as those lanterns danced on the breeze. "¡Adios, Papá! ¡Adios!" Good lord, there wouldn't have been a dry eye on the hill.

And then, if only Caía had placed her hand on the small of Nick's back and slid it around to his side, gently encouraging him to turn around. Maybe then she might have wrapped her arms around him, and kissed him, and said, "I forgive you. Can you ever forgive me?"

Who knows where things might have gone from there.

There was so much to say... so many confessions to make. So much talking to be done, but her father would have said, "Milcz i całuj." *Don't talk. Just kiss.*

He might have also said, "Gdyby kózka nie skakała, to by nózki nie złamała," which loosely translated meant, "If the goat didn't jump, she wouldn't break a leg." In the very same breath, he might have also said, "If the goat didn't jump, she would have a miserable life."

So, which was true?

Both.

Whatever, a broken leg was an easy enough price to pay for a happy life. *Right?*

But there were so many "what ifs." Such as, what if Caía had paid more attention to her son? What if she had said no when he'd asked to go to the park? What if Gregg had never given him that cell phone? What if she had never called him from the bar? What if Jack had never picked up his phone? What if Nick hadn't been on his way home at just the right time?

And later, what if she had never followed Nick to Spain? What if she had never approached Marta that day in the mercado?

What if she had sat home and cried and cried and cried, and never left her bed? What if her mom hadn't died? What if her father wasn't so heartsick after her death? What if Caía had been at his side, holding his hand as he passed from this life to the other, to join his wife and son? What if Caía never pressed Gregg into moving to Chicago? What if they had never even gotten married?

Well, Jack, you wouldn't have been born . . .

It was so easy to imagine how this story should unfold.

Relationships don't thrive on lies. So, what else can you do but move on, go home—make a new life, because the life you left already feels strange. Hopefully, you walk away changed, with the understanding that we all exist on borrowed time. You make the most out of life, with the simple knowledge that even if life isn't fair, death is. It comes for everyone eventually, and every story ends the same way . . . whether you're a little boy in Poland waiting for his mom and dad to bring him home . . . or a little girl in Athens, Georgia, who thinks the sun revolves around her.

But this could be another ending: Her father also used to say, "Swój ciągnie do swojego." *Same kinds attract.* What if living things are bound by the energy that surrounds us? What if we can change the course of our lives by listening to the right frequencies? What if nothing is a coincidence and everything is connected? Even those strange, little exploding cucumbers . . .

"Stella, no!" Caía shouted.

Seizing her four-year-old cousin by the hand before she could touch one of the dischargeable green pods, Laura said, "Don't worry, Tiíta, I have her."

At twelve, Laura was already becoming a little lady, wearing hoop earrings that made her face look too mature. She'd lost her baby fat and was dressed like a little hipster, with a Star Wars backpack looped over one shoulder. Her mom walked ahead, with a new boyfriend, an Italian who seemed secure enough in their relationship to allow Marta to come here and celebrate her ex-husband.

Nick rushed up, scooping their daughter into his arms. He placed Stella upon his shoulders. "Check it out," he said, pointing to an eagle flying near eye level. "Eagle," he said. "Bird."

Stella kicked his chest, bouncing happily on his shoulders. "Agua," she said, pointing instead to the lake sparkling like diamonds below.

Laura launched into a history lesson, one-upping her uncle. "Uncle Nick? Remember, you said el Torre del Homenaje was built in the thirteenth century, well it wasn't, you know. The castle was built on top of an older eighth century Nasrid watchtower. Only later it was used by el casa de León, and that's when they named it the tower of tribute."

"Cool," Nick said, speaking her language, and Laura immediately changed topics.

"Can we go swimming later? La playita is open and Pepi said there are lifeguards over there and you can see your feet on the bottom, clear as can be."

"Sure, why not," Nick said, but he looked at Caía. "Okay with you?"

"Of course," she said. "If it's all right with Marta, it's fine with me." And then she stopped, turning around long enough to take in her surroundings.

Five years had changed so much.

This high up, it seemed as though they must be closer to God. It was impossible not to see the beauty surrounding them and not know there was something bigger. The sky was so damned blue. The clouds so puffy and light. For just one moment, even the wind stilled, as though the world itself held a reverent breath. It was here she felt most at one with the Universe.

Right here.

Caía resisted the urge to pull her cell phone out of her pocket, to photograph the view, staying in the moment.

Hey, Ma . . .

Caía smiled.

There you are, Jack.

Nice gear.

Caía peered down at her hiking boots. Hardcore, with nice treads. Nick had picked them out for her. The house in Jeréz was filling up fast. There was a full-time nursery, and they only just moved Stella into her own room. Caía patted her belly, peering down at the wedding band on her left hand, a simple band engraved with each of their names on the underside.

Caía had decided to pursue a career as a professional interpreter. She was now fluent in Spanish, English, and Polish, and was adding French, Italian, and German to her list.

On the other hand, Nick still hadn't figured out what he wanted to do. He was too content with his roles as uncle and dad, and he still walked Laura to school every day. The money he'd earned in Chicago was well-invested, and Caía didn't foresee that he would be in any hurry to make a different decision anytime soon. By the choices he made, he reminded her daily of the things that were important. *You would like him*, she said to Jack, and knew it would be true.

If her son had to go the way he did . . . there was comfort in knowing Nick's eyes were the last he'd met. She understood, firsthand, what that felt like, and she knew what her son must have seen in the depth of Nick's eyes . . .

Everything's gonna be all right, Ma.

Caía inhaled a breath, and Nick came up behind her, placing a hand around her waist, patting her belly but saying nothing, pulling her close. Stella's shoe tangled itself in her hair.

A cell phone rang, the sound distant and muffled, and neither Caía nor Nick moved to answer, or even to check to see who was calling.

The ring fell silent, and then all she could hear was the sound of breathing, the rustling of leaves, and an eagle squawk, like the punctuation of a sentence without words, and the occasional squeaking of the rubber sneaker tangled in her hair.

☙

Acknowledgments

Heartfelt acknowledgments to Rose Hollander, Eric Gerstner and Mary Beth and Mike Acosta, whose fellowship in Spain enriched *Redemption Song*.

And also to Jose Maria, whose lovely home was an inspiration, even if the details have changed.